Praise for *Follow Me to Ground*

"A wildly imaginative exploration of desire, fear, and what it means to be a person . . . Beautiful and terrifying."

—*The Times* (UK)

"The importance of subtlety is underrated in horror fiction. . . . Sue Rainsford understands this truth, and that's one reason her first novel, *Follow Me to Ground*, leaves such a powerful impression. Never overexplaining the strange world in which she places her characters, she builds a growing sense of dread with chilling images, poetic language, and an eerie, hypnotic rhythm."

—*Newsday*

"Part fairytale, part myth, with a touch of horror and a heavy dose of magical realism, [*Follow Me to Ground*] is unsettling in the best way. Ada's otherness allows us to see human illness at a remove and to consider what it might mean to be truly healed."

—*Electric Literature*

"Compelling . . . Ada may be nonhuman, but Rainsford's lyrical, hypnotic prose allows us to relate to her with ease. There is a furtiveness in the book, both in story and style, with Rainsford artfully bringing the reader along even as Ada's desires grow ever more dangerous."

—*The Irish Times*

"Sue Rainsford's fresh and exciting first novel, *Follow Me to Ground*, reads like a dark fairy tale. . . . a pleasure to read. Seeing the world from Ada's perspective is intoxicating, and as she grows in her power, we feel lucky to be taken along for the ride. With language that's visceral and jarringly beautiful, Rainsford has created a mysterious world that left me wanting to hear more tales of the strange healers and their trusting Cures."

—*BookPage*

"In this serenely haunting tale, told in prose at once lyrical and unsettling, a lonely inhuman girl running a magical curing business with her father searches for a way to come alive. . . . Visceral in its descriptions and carried by a spellbinding first-person narrative intertwined with lore from fearful Cures, this unworldly story is a well-crafted and eerie exploration of desire . . . beautifully intoxicating."

—*Shelf Awareness*

"As the world around us becomes more frightening, we're seeing fiction reflect those terrors, becoming more expansive in its speculative, magical, and often apocalyptic themes; Sue Rainsford's debut falls directly into this camp. It's as much about our difficulty connecting with others as it is about family, community, and compassion. . . . *Follow Me to the Ground* is deeply rooted in human flesh, bodies, and transformation."

—*Thrillist*

"Rainsford draws readers into her arresting and disconcerting tale. . . . *Follow Me to Ground* is a haunting and puzzling story ~~that is~~ ~~afraid~~ to poke about the horror that can exist within an individua~~l~~ Rainsford's earthy tale."

"This wildly inventive story reads like a never heard before, and [Rainsford's] pro

"*Follow Me to Ground* is a haunting, intoxicating debut that establishes its author as one to watch in the future."

—*BookBrowse*

"An astonishing debut heralding the career of an exciting new writer. Strange, lyrical, and arresting, this novel will draw readers into its extraordinary spell."

—*Kirkus Reviews* (starred review)

"In this exhilaratingly original work, lyrical prose gives voice to the strange and alluring Ada, whose spellbinding account alternates with the Cures' testimonials. Seductive and finally horrific; highly recommended."

—*Library Journal* (starred review)

"Brimming with dark folklore and underworld energy, Rainsford's stellar debut features a memorable heroine chafing against her monstrous isolation. . . . Rainsford excels in describing the grotesque beauty of . . . alternative medicine in which the humming healers feel their 'way to the pitch of [the patient's] hurt.'. . . This is a subtle, unsettling novel in which desire is an ineradicable sickness that can be preferable to health."

—*Publishers Weekly* (starred review)

"Haunting . . . With an evocative novel bending fantasy into a universe of subtle horror and bodies cracking open to be healed, Rainsford pulls the reader into a frightening, tangible world of monstrosity, humanity, and healing."

—*Booklist*

"Sue Rainsford's *Follow Me to Ground* is a triumph of imagination and myth-bending—a weird, tender, haunted, and deeply affecting spectacle, equal parts beauty and horror, and unlike anything you will read this year."

—Téa Obreht, author of *The Tiger's Wife* and *Inland*

"A tangled, gnarled, wonderfully original, strange, beautiful beast of a book. I will be reading everything Rainsford ever writes."

—Daisy Johnson, author of *Everything Under* and *Sisters*

"Sue Rainsford has written a gorgeous and unsettling novel. *Follow Me to Ground* is a fresh and primal exploration of bodies and healing, of the fight between one's calling and most ardent desires. A stunningly original debut."

—Megan Mayhew Bergman, author of *Birds of a Lesser Paradise* and *Almost Famous Women*

"Sue Rainsford's *Follow Me to Ground* carries both the great force of myth and the clarity of song. In Ada, her father, and in their shape-shifting, unforgettable journey, we are given a merciless chronicle of this bright, wounded world. This is a novel that burns beautifully, that dives to levels we are blind to, and soars."

—Paul Yoon, author of *Once the Shore* and *The Mountain*

"Sue Rainsford's talent is fierce, palpable, and hypnotic. . . . a dazzlingly troubling dream."

—Colin Barrett, author of *Young Skins*

FOLLOW ME TO GROUND

A NOVEL

SUE RAINSFORD

SCRIBNER

New York   London   Toronto   Sydney   New Delhi

Scribner
An Imprint of Simon & Schuster, Inc.
1230 Avenue of the Americas
New York, NY 10020

This book is a work of fiction. Any references to historical events,
real people, or real places are used fictitiously. Other names,
characters, places, and events are products of the author's imagination, and any
resemblance to actual events or places or persons,
living or dead, is entirely coincidental.

Copyright © 2018 by Sue Rainsford
Originally published in 2018 in Ireland by New Island Books

All rights reserved, including the right to reproduce this
book or portions thereof in any form whatsoever.
For information address Scribner Subsidiary Rights Department,
1230 Avenue of the Americas, New York, NY 10020.

First Scribner trade paperback edition January 2021

SCRIBNER and design are registered trademarks of The Gale Group, Inc.,
used under license by Simon & Schuster, Inc., the publisher of this work.

For information about special discounts for bulk purchases,
please contact Simon & Schuster Special Sales at 1-866-506-1949
or business@simonandschuster.com.

The Simon & Schuster Speakers Bureau can bring authors
to your live event. For more information or to book an event contact
the Simon & Schuster Speakers Bureau at 1-866-248-3049
or visit our website at www.simonspeakers.com.

Interior design by Kyle Kabel

Manufactured in the United States of America

1   3   5   7   9   10   8   6   4   2

Library of Congress Cataloging-in-Publication Data: https://lccn.loc.gov/2018400595

ISBN 978-1-9821-3363-4
ISBN 978-1-9821-3364-1 (pbk)
ISBN 978-1-9821-3365-8 (ebook)

For Angie, cool hand on my brow
For Ali, deep breath in my lungs
For Pat, iron flecks in my will
And for Conor, hot blood of my heart.

PART I

The summers here are made of long, untended grass and flat, lemon light. Baking ground. Sunshine-haze. Shadows cast so dark and deep they seem as solid and alive as the bodies that throw them.

The summers here see even the mornings sharp with heat, and every morning I leave the hot mess of my sheets to stand outside on the patio stones and study the drain.

This gullied, gutted hole.

Even now it sparkles with its secret wet supply.

I'm fearful of it.

The drain.

Fearful because no matter how long and dry the summer, slugs come up the drain and creep on their snake-bellies 'round the patio, trying to get into the house.

I've hated slugs since I was a child. Once, I pinched one between my forefinger and thumb and rubbed it to death. It was a baby, no larger than a bean.

At night I hear their slow procession, all the slugs that live beneath the house. I hear them moving around, shriveling over the pebbles and dirt like the skin on staling fruit. Wandering blindly up and down the lawn. Stalk-eyes roving.

Now, in the daytime, the garden is all rustle and sigh and I can't hear whatever sounds their lithe bellies might be making.

I see one, its blind snout appearing—a thumb-sized black snake departing the rim of the cracked drain's edge. It heads for the dry grass that sits like crust overcooked around the lush innards of the lawn.

If Father were here he'd scatter salt.

He'd pour it down the drain.

If I'd the stomach for the sizzle and stink their thousand corpses would make I'd do the same.

Father didn't hate slugs, but he was wary of them.

Liquid and solid, they're neither one thing nor the other, and they take their time in coming.

It's fitting, I suppose, that I should be tracking one today. This day that sees a long wait come to a close. Because The Ground is moving.

For the first time in all these long, pale years. It's moving.

It's finished; done.

Nearby the lavender, grown in a heap, has had its scent worn away.

Such is the way in this heat.

Little keeps.

Little, that is, aboveground.

PART II

Father was always more creaturely than me.

There were nights when he'd let his spine loosen and go running on all fours through the woods, leaving sense and speech behind.

He'd come back 'round dawn, his throat and his chest and his belly smeared with red, pushing in the back door and straightening up in the kitchen. Bones clicking, shoulders rolling into place, he'd say

—Why don't you ever come hunt with me, Ada?

And I'd laugh and remind him that I'd pleasures all my own.

Every morning when we were expecting a Cure, he'd say

—You've a Cure today, Ada.

As if he needed to remind me. As if I'd ever once forgot. I'd be kneeling in the grass, getting familiar with a cricket or a bird, and he'd call to me—just for the satisfaction, it sometimes seemed, of disrupting me: *Cure today, Cure today . . .*

This particular morning it couldn't have been long after six but already the summer heat was settling in, the sky wide and bleached, and The Ground calling for rain.

The garden is long and mostly grass but back then, close to the house, we kept a patch of moist, fragrant soil. This was as much ground as Father had managed to tame, and it was where we put Cures that needed long, deep healing. The easier ones we saw to in the house. The rest of The Ground we didn't use for anything; it was too temperamental and kept to rules we couldn't follow. The Burial Patch let Cures sleep their sickness away—sped up stitch and suture—but The Ground, the long, long lawn, it gorged on bodies. Shaped them to its own liking.

The Ground is where Father and I were born. It appears randomly, in all sorts of places, and so though Father was born in The Ground he was born somewhere else, somewhere far away.

Inside the house Father was bent over the stove, stewing a broth that had a citrus smell. He was so tall and had to bend so deep it often struck me he'd have been better kneeling. His faded white shirt and his faded white pants gave his skin a sandy sparkle. When it was hot enough to sweat he glowed against the dull house, against the cracked porcelain and the faded pine and the rugs whose colors looked like they'd been watered down.

I nodded at the broth.

—Is that for Mrs. Levine?

Claudia Levine was that day's Cure.

—No, it's not for anyone. I'm trying something new.

Claudia Levine arrived at noon and I sang her belly open, sang her sickness away—tricked it into a little bowl under the table. Closed her up again, woke her up again. Told her she'd be sore in the morning, waved her away down the drive, poured her sickness down the drain.

And then I went out to meet Samson.

Such was the easy, singsong pattern of my days.

Often, a Cure would say *You probably don't remember me but I'm Such-and-Such's daughter* and we'd say *Oh yes we do of course we do* while recalling some unspectacular mother or father, and they'd look at us long and wistful, hoping for some little glimmer of our private selves.

We tried not to get too personal with Cures or let them see too many of our ways. They scared easy, and while they knew that we didn't eat and that we aged slow, they didn't know I stole the song out of baby birds or that Father ran through the woods like a bear.

No. Most Cures frightened easy.

That was part of the magic about Samson.

I'd been seeing Samson for what felt like a long time, mostly because I couldn't remember how I'd gotten by without him.

He'd come to the house a few months before, looking to be cured of a sore on the roof of his mouth. I almost laughed at the smallness of it—it seemed such a harmless, nonsense thing to pay for—but he said it'd been there for weeks with no sign of going away. I didn't even need to put him asleep, just made him rest his head back in the kitchen chair and sang a little tune into his open mouth. I held his head and hooked my thumbs into his cheeks, and later he told me that was what did it. The sore came up on the wall behind him because I'd been too lazy to fetch a cup or bowl. It puckered there, discoloring the paint, while he looked at me and said he liked the sound of my name.

This is something Cures don't know about their curing.

The sickness isn't gone.

It just goes elsewhere.

Late the day after, Annabelle Lennox arrived with two lungs full of fluid that couldn't be tended to while still inside her, so we took them out and put her to ground.

First, we laid her on the kitchen table and unbuttoned her dress—like she was already a corpse we meant to bathe.

Her ribs had dark, smudged shadows between them, like they'd been whitewashed with paint and the undercoat was starting to wear through. I was holding two hands over her face and singing—clucking whenever it looked like she might waken.

Father opened her quickly, his large hand disappearing inside her with a papery sound. He studied the left lung and then the right. She gasped, coarsely, when he lifted them out of her. He went to the pantry holding one in each hand. Their mucus trailed behind him, catching on corners. Wispy. Smoky. I heard him go out the patio door and then saw him through the kitchen window: digging.

He came back in, wiping his hands on his shirt.

—All right.

He lifted her and I held her head so her neck didn't pull, slipping my fingers under her curls. Soft warm scalp.

She looked much smaller, laid out in the hole Father had made for her. This was often the case.

The juice of her innards still clung to Father's forearms with a slow, thick shine.

The mouth of the shovel caught the last of the evening light as he filled in the hole. Quick, practiced motion. The handle worn smooth where he gripped it. A high wind was rolling in, shaking the oleander and making the lamp over the patio door squeak. It was night, all of a sudden, and I was tired.

Miss Lennox's dress had turned the color of the damp ground. Now, almost covered up, she started to kick a little, her bare heels scuffing at the walls of her shallow bedding.

All this time I could hear her lungs—rocking inside the pantry, a sound like a boat tied at harbor. When the hole was filled Father walked across it in careful, even steps, pressing the soil down smooth.

He was very particular, when it came to digging.

Father started giving me slow drips of warning about The Ground when I was only a few weeks old.

—If it takes you there's not much you can do. Try not to squirm and keep one hand straight up in the air. If you go in over your head, try not to open your mouth and eyes. No matter how long you're there for, keep your face shut up tight.

—But you'll see me?

—I'll see you.

—And you'll get me right away?

—There's no reason for you to be in that part of the garden without me, anyway. Especially not before, during, or after rain.

—But we're from The Ground.

—We are, and it would take us back if it could.

It never took me, though I was out there for almost half of every day. Trying to keep myself company.

I'd no one like myself other than Father, who was always working, and I frightened the Cure children. First time I tried to lie down with a boy, I didn't know what I was doing. I lay down and he lay down over me and I held on tight. He went to put it in and there was nowhere for it to go and he got scared and bit me. Right on the neck. Left me with a toothy rosy ring and my smock creased 'round my thighs. Ran back to the house and to his mother, who Father was busy curing. I looked up through the branches and tutted, wondering at the sweet-hurt ache I know now to be what Cures call "lust," "longing."

By the time I took Samson inside, I'd grown myself an opening that I'd a dozen names for. The longing had come on strong enough by then, and so it appeared:

my glove

my pucker

my pouch

The first time was a week after I'd cured him. I'd been thinking about the soft fuzz of his hair on the back of his head and the strong tendons run up his throat.

I was walking toward Sister Eel Lake and the day was scalding. The long grass at the side of the dirt road yellow and chafing and all the trees wilting.

—Miss Ada? That you?

He'd parked his truck off the road, deep in shade. I could see him leaning on the door, an arm resting on the mirror at the driver's side. I said

—What are you doing out here?

Knowing there was nothing between the Cures' village and our home. He had on a white vest that his sweat saw stick to him. I looked at his chest and its nest of hair. He was leaning on the side of the truck and now he laughed and rubbed at his hard, taut stomach.

—I thought you might sing to me.

We lay down in the open back of the truck and he asked if there was much chance of hurting me. I only laughed and when I took him inside I laughed again, it was that good a feeling.

And so, quickly, we got into the habit of one another.

Henry Law

It was easy to forget they're not like us.

You could be looking at Miss Ada and talking to her simply, and then she'd say something like

Take into account the evenings are getting long, Mr. Law.

Her father too. We'd be talking easily enough and then all of a sudden I'd remember he knew my pop and all my uncles from the day they were born till the day they died.

I suppose it was easy to forget because they made it easy. They had to, to get by.

It didn't matter to Father that most Cures were cautious of us because he didn't care for company, and it didn't matter to him that a couple of the curings became local folklore and got told over and over, getting longer and stranger each time.

Tabatha Sharpe, for instance.

She was a Cure of mine from when I was very young and first in the habit of going for walks near Sister Eel Lake. I'd play in the long pale grass, pulling it around myself and weaving a wheaten cradle. I laced the stalks over one another into thick and clumsy plaits in the way that some Cure women bound their hair, and lay there for an hour or so, imagining myself an infant Cure. Helpless. Speechless. Pursing my mouth to signal I wanted my mother's teat.

Father had told me that Cures remember nothing of being inside their mothers, which I thought strange. I remembered so clearly my time in The Ground. I remembered the closeness of the soil and the taste of rain come down toward me.

Once the backs of my legs started itching I kicked away the cradle.

Shredded its walls.

Tore it down.

On the way home I played a game I often played when lazy with heat. It was a simple game: I'd look into Sister Eel Lake and convince myself I saw her there—whiskery, oily mouth—and so frighten myself into running all the way home.

I squatted in the rushes and felt my dress peel away from my back, waiting to be taken by surprise.

But then: a noise. A real noise. A noise I hadn't spun in my head.

A wet, slipping sound, and a pocket of air dispersing.

There was a baby where there hadn't been one before. A baby wrapped in a bit of cloth torn from a sheet or a large man's shirt. The cloth was covered in stringy bits of blood and the baby was sickly. I lifted it into my lap and the small head rolled away.

Tiny throat. Too tiny to cry.

Little pink disk for a face, the features slightly flattened.

Fair hair plastered down with mucus and blood.

I checked it over and saw it was a girl.

My first thought: *Some crazed parent has left her here for Sister Eel.*

Offerings were sometimes made to her by Cures who thought she could shimmy under the fields and make succulent the crops, though it was usually a calf or a fox they left for her.

With my arms around the baby I walked the quarter hour home, looking at her face.

Mouth like a berry still ripening.

Eyelids so thin I could see through them.

We'd no Cures scheduled that day, and so I knew there'd been an accident when I saw the old van parked at a hard, quick angle to the house.

A smell of wet was coming off the van, a sucked-penny smell, and once inside the house it wafted thick and strong. I followed it upstairs, an ache starting in my arms with the weight of the baby. I could hear Father talking.

They were in the third spare room—our best room, with its view of the garden's greenest part. There was a woman in the rocking chair. She was crying, mostly with pain, and there was a man crying with sadness behind her. Father was on his knees. He said

—You really mustn't move.

I'd never seen the woman before but later learned her name: Mrs. Delilah Sharpe. She was sat in the rocking chair and her dress was rolled up to her waist and she held her own knees very far apart. Father was rolling a strip of torn sheet to pad at the soreness between Mrs. Sharpe's legs—there was already a heap of used ones on the ground, and I clucked my tongue at the long chore ahead of me: washing the strips one by one; perhaps even stitching the sheet up again.

Mr. Sharpe saw me first, and then Father turned around. Mrs. Sharpe lay back in the chair, her eyes closing.

The sun had gotten higher and the day was pumping hot and cruel outside.

—I found her at Sister Eel Lake.

Father had come close to me, stopped when he could see the baby's wrinkled head. She seemed heavier, now that I was standing still, and squirmed while I did my best to rock her.

—Should I boil up some daisies?

Which was a broth we made for damaged parts.

—Go give Mrs. Sharpe her baby, Ada.

By now Mrs. Sharpe was trying to right herself in the chair. Mr. Sharpe was still crying but not making any sound.

—You do it.

I held her up to Father and he looked at me stone-hard, slit-eyed.

19

A scolding later. For sure.

He took her from the sullied cloth and carried her to Mrs. Sharpe. When she reached across her risen stomach, more bright blood came out of her. I heard its soft drip on the rug. Mr. Sharpe sat down on the floor, his back to the wall. They were a young couple, and probably not married long.

I stayed in the door moving from one foot to the other, wringing out the cloth, until I noticed the copper flecks on my hands. Like I'd been clutching a rusty pipe.

—I best get this in the bath before the stains stick.

But I was well forgotten by now.

I don't know if Father ever realized how this story spread in the town. Cures couldn't grasp that a baby could leave its mother without being birthed, could wind up so far away and be discovered by me. As though plucked out of the air. It made more sense to them that I'd killed the Sharpe baby and given her parents a changeling—a strange little creature like myself, who would someday do my bidding.

For years I wondered if it was my dream of a cradle that called her to me. This was better than thinking that Sister Eel Lake was simply where too-soon babies go.

Always when we met he'd have some quick greeting ready. The third time we saw one another, the day after we put Miss Lennox to ground, he said

—You get on better with the heat.

It was the first time I'd gotten into the front of the truck. The edges of the passenger seat were stained a deep brown. He had Cure music playing and it seemed to gather speed as he turned corners and cast backward glances at the road by way of the little mirror between us. The bottom of the window had the usual hillside pattern of dust thrown up by wheels and missed by wipers.

We came to Sister Eel Lake and he looked at me.

—Keep driving.

I was surprised he'd been willing to stop there. Almost everyone was cautious of the lake and believed the story of the cannibal serpents. Those giant, gorging eels grown during the war to kill enemy soldiers who stopped to bathe and swim. It was well known how they'd gone hungry some weeks into peacetime, and so began to swallow one another whole.

When only Sister and Brother Eel remained they watched one another until the brother fell asleep, and it was his fear that shook me, *his* fear upon waking. Thrashing in the tight dark that was his sister, engulfed even as he stirred from sleep.

It was Sister Eel who had years ago eaten most of Christopher Plume, a slim and freckled child, when he was nine. Father worked on him a great deal, out of courtesy to the family.

—Are you afraid of your father seeing us?

Driving under a willow tree whose branches snagged around the windows.

—Father doesn't really leave the house.

This was part of a lie we kept afloat. Cures would scare easy at Father's animal tendencies, blame him for livestock gone missing, though he never hunted anything that wasn't wild.

We kept going and came to wider, more unkempt corners.

—I heard that. I didn't think it was true.

—He doesn't feel the need.

We came through a brief density of trees and the road straightened.

—But you do.

—I like the change in air.

His thighs clenched inside his trousers. I looked out the window, said

—There's always a lot of smells in our house.

He was swallowing from thirst. I stopped talking. We came to the river.

—How about here?

He left the truck parked by a high bush grown up straight and thick like a wall. We'd arrived by the main road, not the back paths I usually walked down. The trees on the river's far side were maybe fifty feet tall and the branches reached out to criss and cross with their neighbors to make a cool, echo-filled chamber high up in the air. I got out of the truck and shook out my dress, walked toward the reeds. I heard him following me, making the long grass crackle. I said

—I like the river.

—I've never seen you here.

—Father doesn't like me to be seen outside the house.

—Why's that?

—I suppose it's not so important now. It was more for when I was a child and Cures weren't sure what to make of me.

—Cures? He laughed. That's what you call us?

He was walking alongside me now and I watched his vest catch at the top of his trousers, twisting and releasing with his long high strides. We reached the shade and it felt like stepping through a wall of water. I felt him looking at me. My smock, hanging free of one shoulder, was clinging to my stomach and the short prickling hair on my groin.

—Were you really so strange?

—There were certain things about me.

By which I meant my girlhood, constant and unceasing.

A Cure could live their whole lifespan and never notice a change in me, and so, to them, I seemed a girl of sorts forever.

There wasn't a way I didn't want to swallow him whole. Not only up 'tween my legs but down my throat. The feel of him moving over me and our thighs skimming, our stomachs sealed tight. I'd opened up so many Cures but couldn't think what he had inside him that would let him build this fire in me, this tingling that built and built until I thought it'd tear me apart. Couldn't think how I'd changed so much in so short a time that I wanted it so badly, to be torn.

Later we rested beside one another in the grass. I kept looking up at the knotted branches and the thin slivers of blue where they let through the sky. I touched his head, his too-soft curls. He was tired, half dreaming.

—I was a long time in the desert.

And then he laughed at himself. But I knew what he meant.

It was late at night two days later when we went out to fetch Miss Lennox. When the air hit her she turned hummingbird: finger-tap, tremble-knee. Father carried her into the kitchen and we laid her out again. It took time enough to open her, with her being stilled so long in The Ground. The skin was all stiff and cold.

—She'll scar, I said, and Father nodded.

I went to fetch the lungs. They rocked and swished slowly inside of the bowl, their mucus sticking to my fingers and wrists. It sometimes happened that the halted stillness worked into a Cure and their parts colored the air around them. It generally went unnoticed by Cures themselves, but it was possible to see on occasion a slight slowing of time—a wound appearing in some soft flesh but not coloring with blood. This was why the skein off Miss Lennox's lungs took its time in rising and its time in falling. Where it touched me it left behind a cringing, grisly sensation.

The night was cool but Father's chest was shining with sweat. Lungs were always tricky.

Her insides were filling the room with a sound of water. A lake lapping against its edges and shifting the pebble and grit.

I handed Father the first lung, and after he'd placed it inside her I did the detail work—the work his hands were too big for, stoppering and making seamless frayed holes and cords. Undoing as best I could all the strangeness her thin body had seen.

The second lung took quicker, squirming from Father's hand and filling the space it had left behind. We closed her then and bathed the blood away, and Father woke her.

Her mother arrived to collect her at a quarter past three in the morning as she'd been told. Father walked Miss Lennox out to the car and I stood in the door, letting the nighttime cool settle 'round me.

They drove off. The car was an old one and sputtered, coughed. The headlamps were covered with dust from the road and gave off only a little light.

Father was walking his slow gait. From the middle of the drive he said

—Time for bed now, Ada.

—Might sleep late in the morning.

And then he walked past me, his arm grazing mine. I kept on looking out at the night. The moonshine was making silver the top of a tree that kept rustling, on and off, with the red-tailed hawk that nested there.

There are some technical terms around curing:

declension

auscultate

Father made me learn them but we never used them, not even to one another. I think teaching them to me was just another way to fill up the days.

He wrote poems for me, which worked better—small, simple verses to help me understand the work we did.

> *lest you tumble, slip,*
> *or trip!*
> *Hold firm, not tight, and*
> *lift with both hands, however light!*

I'd murmur them aloud while pulling weeds from The Ground or scrubbing strips of linen, but it took me a long time to fathom the long line of ailments ahead of me.

Chafed skin and chalky bones.

Too-thin veins and too-large hearts.

Every now and then Samson would talk about his sister, the recently widowed Olivia, how they'd grown up in a small room in their aunt's house. How Olivia hated what she called "the poverty," hated the whole town.

—When we were little she thought the only way she'd escape was the circus, but then she started meeting men. And then she met Harry. But then, Harry's house was so big, I don't think she knew what to do with all the different rooms.

He was sitting under a tree, shirtless in the shade, watching me wade in the river. For something to say, I said

—Harry was much older than her.

I'd cured him, one time, for a bitter bile in his stomach.

—She wanted to get married quick, before she had to work. She wouldn't last a day in the fields.

—And what does she do with the rooms, now that he's died?

He made a noise in his throat.

—His parents kicked her out, so she's living with me again.

Which was their aunt's house, the house they'd grown up in and which their aunt had left to Samson when she died.

I knelt in the water. It came up my shoulders, slipped under my hair.

—Do you have the space?

—Hardly. We're back sharing a bed, like when we were children. See?

26

And he turned around, showed me where her knees had left bruises down his back.

Sometimes we didn't go to the river but into the woods, deep into its middle where the branches gathered in knots and hid us from the hot blue sky. It needed constant tending: Samson's skin the sun might set to singing, Samson's want of shelter, Samson's want of cool.

Often, when it came time to lie down together, he'd already be pink and dazed—weighted down by the sun. I caught myself at such times, thinking how little it'd take to open him, to be inside him and see how compact, how snug, and how *sound* the mechanisms therein.

A warm sweep across my pelvic floor. A long exhale down my spine.

A heat kept just off the boil.

Lilia Gedeo

I've stomach problems, you see.

That and a tightness in the chest come springtime—the pollen! Yes, the pollen. It seems to stick to my throat.

So I was always up there, when I was young. Can't count how many times I was put to ground. All that soil—and it was a different kind of soil. It never quite came out in the wash.

But I didn't mind. Of course I didn't mind.

I was just happy to have been made *well*!

Whether it was my stomach or my lungs. Or one of my headaches. I get desperate headaches too.

We've a man now that comes around the houses, since Miss Ada stopped curing. He comes around with his bag of tricks, and oh, it just isn't the same.

When Mr. Kault came to see us his neck was all bruised. Father said he must have been kneading himself, trying to loosen the knot at the base of his skull from his cerebellum growing twisted and hard.

Cerebellum.

Sarah-balloon.

Sear-bloom.

Edible-sounding, the name itself full of swell. Apparently supple when healthy.

We put him to sleep in the sitting room and then rolled him facedown on the couch. I held his thumb in my hand.

He was the only man I'd ever seen of similar size to Father, though even as he lay still in the afternoon light I could see him shedding flake after flake of skin while all Father ever parted with was the mark of his mouth on his mug, maybe the fleeting indent of his hand on a Cure.

We'd opened him just enough to spy the withered, partial organ.

—There's not that much to be done. This hard grind of muscle, we can bring that down. But the problem is deeper. Something we can't fix.

—Why can't we fix it?

—Because sick is sick, and it has to go somewhere, and some sicknesses are dangerous when taken out of a body.

By which he meant madness and perversion. Seeing as he let Mr. Kault in the house I assumed it was madness. Maybe the glitching memory or the many-voices kind.

—And sometimes, even though it's harmful, if a sickness has been deep-set too long a body doesn't think to expel it.

—How d'you mean?

—It takes a toll on the flesh it's leaving.

I looked at him blank though it irked him when I didn't catch his meaning right away. He looked from me back to Mr. Kault's sore neck and said

—I mean if it's left untended too long the body can't live without it.

Sitting back on my ankles I imagined a small lamb come into the room and trying to suckle on me, moving its rough tongue from left to right. At first I didn't know why, but then I remembered: Mr. Kault's cousin, Lorraine Languid. Some fifteen or so years before. It was the only time Father and I had together left the house, to the farm where Mr. Languid lived with his wife and sons. Lorraine Languid was a young woman still and I was slowly finishing being a child. Father had made the rare exception to tend to a Cure in his own home, and to distract herself Lorraine took me to the barn. The lambs were there, and the hay was all slick with their pursing mouths. I remember Lorraine tried to hold my hand, and I'd made it into a fist and tried to shake away the feel of her holding it. That curing had been a strong one. It gave Mr. Languid another five years (at which point his heart would again make that smacking sound, but he'd be far away and not found until the bonnet of his truck had cooled). Father was at his strongest then. Even his mildest touch did a lot of good.

We kneaded and kneaded Mr. Kault and then we hummed and sang. When we opened him fully and lifted out the cerebellum it made a harsh, coughing sound. His mouth had leaked its moisture into the sitting room couch, bringing the old pink cushion up in a soft, mauve bruise.

—If we were to try and fix the deep-down sickness, what might we do?

Father shrugged.

—Bleed him. And keep him hidden from the moon. But when a sickness like that leaves the body there's no telling where it will go.

He was quiet a moment, looking at this large man that couldn't be saved.

—If we were risk takers we might put him to ground— The Ground. But there's no way to know for sure what it would do.

—It might cure him?

—Not quite. The Ground flips things around. Either way, he wouldn't be a Cure anymore.

—He'd be more like us?

—He couldn't heal, but he'd be different. On the inside.

We put Mr. Kault in to ground, to the left and farthest corner from the house. We knew he would kick and kick he did. His thighs were broad. A horse's hind leg. Back in the house I listened for the sound of his grave breaking, but it didn't come.

I went to bed, thinking hard on Samson and hoping to sow the seeds of a dream: his stomach coming undone, a wide mouth tasting the air, a sliver spreading up the center of his almond-shell chest.

I wanted to dream of his heart, its beat sullen and low.

His heart that was a crimson heart, not the pastel shades of other Cures.

Snug in my hand, his quadrant muscle.

Feeling it beat against my palm.

But when I closed my eyes, all I could think of was the lambs.

The look of the lambs and their mouths.

The smell of the barn. Lorraine Languid, leaning in the doorway. Putting something in her mouth: a cigarette. Though I didn't know what it was at the time. I thought the smoke was coming from her. I thought her mouth was on fire.

The next morning I went to meet Samson. When I got there he was tanning in the back of his truck, his shirt off and his jeans hanging unevenly around his hips from where he'd pulled the hot buckle away from his skin. I whistled to wake him and climbed into the truck. He scrunched his eyes at me and said

—Must really be summer if you're starting to freckle.

We got into the front, started driving toward the river. He coughed. Looked at my thighs.

—You know I've been hearing 'bout you since I was a boy.

A small insect was scaling the window as we drove. On my side of the glass I followed its trail with my finger, clucking at the thinness of its legs.

—There was a lot of fuss at the time, over Tabatha Sharpe.

Why the Sharpes ever told anyone about how Tabatha came into the world I could never fathom.

—That girl hasn't had the easiest time of it. She was stripped down once, kids looking for teeth marks from Sister Eel.

He waited for me to say something. When I didn't, he said

—Anyway. She was never quite right.

It wasn't the first time I'd heard this kind of talk about Tabatha. Could be I found her too late. Could be too much of the lake was already inside her.

The insect, stripped of its grip as Samson took a corner too sharply, was gone from the window. He kept talking.

—You ever see her?

—Tabatha Sharpe?

—No, Sister Eel.

—No.

Running my hand up the back of my neck, sliding it into my hair. Then, remembering myself,

—Have you?

—No.

Adjusting himself in the seat, trying to lessen contact with the sweating leather,

—But Olivia and I, we used to play a game, if we were ever near the lake.

Which was when their parents were in the fields, before their parents died. Before they went to live with their aunt and slept together in the small creaking bed.

We'd come to the river. Samson turned the key to make the engine hush and then hunched toward the steering wheel. His vest had left a glistening copy of itself behind so that his skin was shining where the droplets sat on his body, thick as tears.

—We'd pretend that we were Brother and Sister Eel and Olivia would chase me, trying to eat me.

His eyes closed. I looked at the cloth of my dress, sticking to me. I lifted it and watched it fall, landing again with a twirl.

—One day we ended up on opposite sides of the lake. Olivia was jumping up and down and saying *I'm gonna catch you and I'm gonna eat you!*

He swallowed and it made a loud clicking sound. He closed his eyes tighter and the skin of his brow bunched toward his eyes.

—I was ducked down in the rushes, and I heard a splash and thought Olivia had fallen in. I saw the spray of water from the ground.

He laughed to himself, said

—Some of it landed in my mouth. I thought I'd die.

Opening his eyes, moving again in his seat.

—So you went looking for Olivia?

—Yes.

He was tense now, like he was bracing against a chill.

—I found her, and she was standing with her hands in her pockets, rubbing her feet in the dirt. Said she'd seen one of the humps, breaking up the water, and then the tail. The tail looked mad, she said. It was the tail that had made the splash.

His eyes were on my knees. Already I felt the scratch of the gorse and grass we'd walk through.

—And Olivia wasn't afraid?

He laughed, moving quickly now, opening the door and swinging his legs outside.

—Olivia doesn't get afraid.

—Not even as a child? Not even of Sister Eel?

—Olivia was never really a child.

Turning back to wink at me.

—Kind of the opposite to you.

And then we were wading through the waist-high grass and his hands were on me like warm water while I opened, spread around him, and held on to him. Whenever he was inside me I turned to a fist, grasping and releasing, a fist learning the shape of the thing it's holding.

Tabatha Sharpe

Only time I met her was when I was born.

Nothing wrong with me my whole life, 'less you count my red-dust-haze. I see red when it rains. When I look at any kind of water—a river or a lake or a stream:

Red

Red

Red

And when people go swimming or stand out in the rain, afterward they're all dripping red.

I didn't realize water wasn't red for everyone else till I was ten and Mother was reading to me from a picture book. I asked her why the rain in the book wasn't red and she was frightened but she kept her fear on the inside like Father can never do.

Just asked me what else was red, and I pointed at her red mouth and her red shoes, and that seemed to calm her.

We never go swimming in the summer, though. And I'm only allowed quick showers, never a bath, and Mother pulls the curtains every time it rains.

Like I said, I was young when Father started feeding me stories and warnings about The Ground.

—The Ground is cruel, but with tilling and culling we can make it useful.

Sitting at the kitchen table, flicking my tongue against the back of my teeth.

—Why only such a small part for burial?

—My father and I worked a long time on taming it just so, so that The Ground would cushion a body and yield it again. Only a small patch can be handled at a time. It takes huge strength. When you are older, we will try to rein in some more. And then, when you have a child, you'll try for more again.

—We don't live here to fix Martha Jacobs?

Miss Jacobs was the pale wisp of a Cure he had seen to that day.

—No, Ada. Had Miss Jacobs lived in a different town, she would have gone unfixed.

—It's about to rain.

A high wind came through the trees. A half mile away I could see the dust on the road shooting up a foot high. Samson said

—We're due a storm.

I was sitting against a tree and he was lying on his shirt.

—Olivia can always tell when rain is coming.

—That right.

Cures often believed themselves a little bit magic. It got tiresome.

—From the smell in the air. Sometimes as far as two days away.

—I see.

—She used to love playing in the rain when we were little. When all the other kids would run inside.

I looked at my feet. Looked at Samson's calves, the left one marked by one long, thin scratch that was filled with wet-dry red. It moved through his fine blond hair with a serpentine twist.

—Anyway. She can tell you about that herself.

I stretched out my own legs. Started thinking about my walk home.

—When would I meet her?

—She's having a baby. Didn't I tell you?

I looked at his face, the side of it not hidden by his arm.

—No. Your sister is pregnant?

—She'll be giving birth soon.

He sat up then, quickly, almost knocking me aside. I pulled my dress toward me while he squatted in the shade, his buttocks made pink and crimson by the brittle twig shards on the ground.

By now it was raining, though it barely made it through the mesh of the trees, landing every now and then on the hot ground with a careful tutting sound.

—So she was pregnant when Harry died?

42

—You can do the math as well as me.

His elbows cut their way through his vest as he pulled it back over his head.

I stood up and headed for the road.

—All right, I said. See you.

—All right. See you.

By the time I got home the sky had a hazardous, silver sheen. I stopped on the bottom step to smell the air. It had that rubbery, skidding-wheel scent that always preceded a storm. I was wet from the rain and the cool felt good to me.

Father was in the sitting room, staring at the angle between the ceiling and the far wall, a mug held in one cupped hand. I said

—Thick rain coming.

This was something we always said when a strong wind came before rain.

Already I could hear the branches tossing themselves against the house and the shutters rattling in their cases. Father would most likely need to turn up his sleeves and see to the leak in the bathroom ceiling. The paint there, flaked and yellowing, garners a slippery shine in the rain. He was a strange sight in the bathroom. It's a low-ceilinged room, and the top of his head grazed the doorframe.

But just now the storm was still cloud-bound and Father's last swill of coffee was losing its grainy scent.

We went to the kitchen. I didn't speak. I was tired and my eyes felt large and unruly in my head. He was talking about our next Cure, Lilia Gedeo. A woman we'd often seen to who'd be coming again soon. He was moving around the countertops, setting the hob alight with its rim of fire-blue.

—What's wrong with her this time?

He kept his back to me. The creases in his shirt were moving like tiny, panicked worms. He was cooking something. On the floor by the table I saw our laundry in a bucket, the linens scrubbed coarse. I sat down and pulled it toward me, started rubbing them off one another, coaxing up suds. I looked up.

—Father?

He shook the pan. A smell of rust and lilac filled the room.

—Where do you go, when you go out during the day?

My dress was sticking to me now.

—Since when does it matter?

—Are you meeting a boy? A man?

—Do I ask you what you do in the woods?

—Ask whatever you like.

—I'd rather do the courteous thing and leave you be.

—I know you meet someone.

My hands quickly turning raw and pink.

I dropped the linens in the water and went outside, out back and onto The Burial Patch, where the weather would stop me hearing him. Before I closed the patio door behind me he called

—You've a Cure tomorrow. Olivia Claudette.

Arson Belle

No one was quite sure what they could and couldn't do——a lot of people thought they could read minds; others thought they could see the future. All that kind of thing. I just went there and asked them to put me straight out. Always said *Do whatever you need to and tell me about it later.*

Once though, he gave me a look like he knew something. After I'd done something I wasn't supposed to. I can say it now, it happened so long ago. I was a young man, didn't know better——and we didn't have many ways to pass the time . . . but a few days later I went to get fixed and he looked at me so long and hard I thought he might hit me. Usually the two of them saw to me, but that time he told Ada to go play. Told her it was too nice a day to be stuck inside.

That night Father went out hunting.

In the kitchen, come evening, he started stirring inside of his clothes.

Things were tense between us but I said

—You go on, I can finish here.

His features suddenly soft with relief, rolling his shirt off his back like it was burning him. The extra length and bend that came into his ankles and wrists always looked like it would pain him.

The arch in his hips.

His shoulders broadening apart.

If it did, he didn't say.

When he came back in the morning he'd a cut down the length of his back. Once he straightened upright again he asked me to dab it with salt. He was too sore to sit down so I had to stand on a chair to reach the top of him.

—Good hunt?

—Yes.

—Deer?

—Yes.

I was out back when I heard Olivia come into the drive. Right away Father was calling to me.

I was standing on The Burial Patch, looking at The Ground. The rain had kept up overnight and the lawn was all grumble and churn. Things were still stiff between Father and me so we didn't speak when I walked through the kitchen. The both of us had tracked in soil and the tiles were marked with swirls of brown.

She was in the sitting room, looking out the window. I followed her gaze and saw she'd come in Samson's truck. I made a noise and she turned to me.

Tall, slim woman. Dark hair and pale skin. Her muscles tight and smooth inside her limbs. From the side of her face I could tell her mouth was set in a hard line but when I said her name and she turned to look at me she melted. Let her shoulders move down her back. Cocked her hip and smiled. This was something I never forgot about her. All tilts, all smiles, but in a practiced kind of way.

—Hello, Mrs. Claudette.

—Oh! Call me Olivia.

—You want me to look at your baby?

A hand on the bottom of her stomach, bearing the weight.

—I've had a pain and some bleeding.

—Heavy or light?

—Heavy at first but now mostly light.

—Why don't you lie back on the couch.

She sat down and made to swing up her legs. I held her beneath the knees and she laughed at the effort it took between us.

—People keep telling me that laughing is bad for the baby, probably because I laugh so hard.

I took off her sandals and placed them near the wall, their barely worn toes nosed into the skirting. She was dark where

Samson was light, though they'd the same fine features, the same dusty shimmer in their eyes.

—Not the case.

She laughed again and I knelt down beside her. Her scent was like Samson's, but sharper.

Her stomach was a high, hard mound. A slim-hipped woman who'd be a long time in birth. I started rolling up her dress and saw her thighs tauten, but someone must have told her what to expect because she lifted her hips and wriggled the dress up to her chest. The panties she had on were bright white, and the slim cloth bridge that covered her lips was only a little sodden and clinging. She must have bathed that morning and been only a short while in her clothes.

There was indeed a bruise.

It started at the left hip and sprawled on her bump's underside. I put a hand over it and my ears filled with a tearing sound. I reached across and slipped my other hand beneath her back, where I heard only a dull whistle. A good sign.

I knew by now she'd be expecting me to speak.

—I'm sorry to hear about your husband, Mrs. Claudette.

—Oh, thank you.

A glance at my hands as they moved around her. And then,

—I'm fine.

The weight of the milk-brew in her breasts made them pull t'ward her face, framing her chin with their topmost bit of bulk.

—I'm going to have a look at the baby now.

Though I said this only to avoid details that might worry her and keep her from sleeping, as I could tell already the baby was fine.

I put a hand over her face. The sweat of her nose and her little mouth, gathered unto itself like a stuffed pouch, left dewy marks on my palm. Without any struggle she was asleep. I ran a finger down the length of her stomach, and the skin was so pliant and young it needed only the gentlest pulling apart.

Her viscera, I could tell, were on a better day all chime.

They'd gotten a shock and the tissue surrounding her womb had grown crimson and tightly wound—but no, it wasn't tissue. Running my fingers over the rivulet mounds, I found it was a layer of tightly packed blood, deeply clotted and in some places already turning to dust.

At this point she took in a few short breaths, which was normal. The lungs raised and steadied but the breath stayed inside her.

Now that she was open the room had filled up with the tearing sound, and the clotting was giving off a smell of blueberries left too long on the stove. I started humming, feeling my way toward the pitch of her hurt. The baby was sleeping; I could see its little shoulders through the curtain of her womb when I lifted the bladder aside.

Once the humming and the tearing blended, I slipped my hand around the clotted blood and clucked at it until it shrank and slid away. It turned from crimson to purple in the shadow of my hand and left her.

Quiet now, aside from the rain. I listened hard: I'd left a bowl under the couch, just in case, but hadn't heard it land there.

I brought the skin back together, smoothing away any puckering with the flat of my hand. It pinkened some, once rejoined, and I waited for the rosiness to fade before waking her. I looked at the clock over the fireplace. It was two in the afternoon.

A very accommodating Cure.

Before coming to her elbows she stared a moment at her stomach in the usual dazed way, mute and uncomprehending, and I helped her roll her dress back down.

—You tore up some tissue, and it bled. You must have fallen or stretched your hip out too far.

She nodded, her mouth a little ways open.

Way, way too far, I thought, and noticed that in tugging on her dress I'd marked it with rusty stains. I wiped my hands on my legs when I hunkered down to pick up her shoes.

—Your baby is working fine. It'll have big green eyes.

I looked her in the face before sliding her sandals back on, feeling the thin bones of her ankles working to flatten her feet. She had thick charcoal lashes and her eyes were the muddied floor of a summertime wood.

—Like its daddy.

She put her hands in mine and pulled, coming to stand. Her face had a hardness to it all of a sudden. Like she'd had when I first came into the room. It stopped her looking like Samson. She said

—Harry didn't have green eyes.

I dropped my hands from hers and opened the door to the hall, calling to Father. Mrs. Claudette didn't move, just stood where I'd left her, perfectly shapen and tall. She was so polished looking. As though her whole life she'd been tended to like a plant that must at all costs flower. And then she was lit up again, a candle flaring behind her eyes, her lips moved by a breathy smile.

—Oh, Miss Ada, I know you know what it's like when a woman's told to earn her keep.

—Well, we all have to work.

—Harry's seed may as well have been water out of the kettle.

She was speaking, rather than whispering, which struck me as strange. I could tell the look she gave me was a rehearsed one, that I was meant to find it hard to look away.

—Mrs. Claudette, who do you think I'm going to tell?

Once they start talking heart and mind, you ask to be paid. So Father always said of Cures who thought us akin to their priests and in the habit of undoing such things as guilt and unseemly longing.

Her face softened and her mouth started moving with quick, unthinking laughter.

—Oh, I know, I know! I'm all worked up—my brother says my hair will fall out if I keep doing the thinking for everyone around me.

—Will your brother be helping you with the baby?

Her eyes darting around my face.

—With your husband gone? Will your brother help you with the baby?

—Oh yes—yes, yes. He has always taken the best care of me.

I made the shape of a smile. Wondered when she'd leave.

—He came here not so long ago. You've a very close scent. Usually takes twinning for siblings to have a scent so close.

But this was too much for her, as allusions to our strangeness often were. She was moving away from me now—

carefully, like she'd just seen a spider or something hungry peering at her from the woods. In my head I saw her hand as she'd have liked to hold it: sheltering her stomach with the fingers flared wide and the skin around the knuckles whitening. She spoke again in a tight little whisper:

—I can't remember a time when we were apart.

By now I was weary of her moods, hopping on the left foot and then back to the right. Father had come out of the kitchen. He looked at me and I nodded and Olivia started asking how we wanted to be paid.

I went outside. A heavy rain had started. I held my elbows and looked out toward the woods from the porch. The rain was coming in straight lines over the edge of the roof and the smell of it soothed me. I could taste the wet bark, the sodden loam.

After a few minutes she came outside, walked down the steps, said some more nonsense I didn't take heed of, turned one more time to wave. She eased herself into the truck, her belly high behind the steering wheel. I watched her drive away, feeling tired and squirmy.

When she was gone I stepped out from under the porch—just enough to feel the water, soft as milk, run down my neck.

In the pantry, picking out leaves to make tea, I found the clot on the third shelf. Shrunken into itself like a kicked cat. Had I been less distracted I'd have buried it properly, rather than taking it outside and simply dropping it on the grass.

Something for The Ground to gnaw on, I said to myself, watching it disappear into the hungry soil.

* * *

The next time we lay down together, Samson was not quite himself. His vest hung wide around his shoulders in a way that made me think he'd slept inside it. The sprawling hair of his armpits was snaky and wet, and his insides were all scented with liquor. I could taste it in the damp of his neck.

He was heavy on top of me, begging me turn over and put my belly in the dirt. He said he wanted to lick my back and I let him, my eyes on the thick bristle-brush.

When he started to sober I could tell his thoughts were full of Olivia, of her thin wrists and her pursing mouth. I said

—You mustn't sicken yourself with worry for your sister.

He was squeezing the flesh on my hips. It hurt and I squirmed, his coarse palms chafing me.

—It'll be an easy birth.

—I know you think the child is healthy.

Feeling the breath of his words where my buttocks met my spine, and then he was leaning back on his heels.

—It is. Healthy.

The bracken dug into my skin. A small spider distinguished itself from the black of the soil.

—You're wrong sometimes.

—When?

He didn't answer. The spider fell to one side, tripped up by a leaf.

—When have I ever been wrong?

I imagined the dim, idle speak of Cures; some insistence that *No, the joint was still not quite right.*

I twisted farther to look at him and saw that his eyes, which had been all afternoon edged with a sore-looking red, had filled with a weak film of water.

—Samson, when have I been wrong?

He swallowed though his mouth was dry.

—With me.

He still held me tight, around my hips, and I thought, vaguely, of later hiding the bruises from Father.

—There's something wrong with me.

—I listened to you closely, Samson. There's nothing wrong.

—I wish that you'd *look*.

—I can't, not without a reason.

My own pleasure not being reason enough.

—But I've asked you.

Which he had, thinking it simply a matter of permission.

His jaw tightened, and the sheen between his lids fractured and spilled.

—Samson, you are *well*.

Still locked between his legs, I had rolled onto my back and reached up, laying a hand flat on his stomach.

—There's no reason for me to lie.

He thought something slippery had gone wrong with him, I could tell that much. Something he knew by feeling but wasn't sure how to say, something he felt certain would show up in the organs and muscles beneath his flesh.

He nodded and took a long breath. Lying down over me again and putting his face in my neck, sleeping.

*   *   *

It's The Ground that brought Father here. There are only so many patches of earth like it. This is one of the reasons we couldn't leave; we couldn't work anywhere else. When I was young and the summer days felt long we'd sit outside and I'd ask him questions he'd already answered:

—Why'd The Burial Patch take so long to tame?

—Because The Ground here is so powerful.

—The Ground is where I came from?

—That's right.

—But not you.

—No. Not this ground.

—And not your father?

—No. Though he is buried here.

And he'd nod to the far left corner, where every other summer a red mold took hold of the trees.

—But you weren't worried making me? Though it's dangerous?

—It was risky, but no. I wasn't worried.

He'd tell me how he mixed my parts together and planted me inside of a sack. He tied it shut with a rope and then lowered me down during a thunderstorm and kept the end of the rope tied to the knob on the patio door.

—Just in case.

—So you *were* worried?

—Not especially. I had a good feeling. And look! You turned out fine.

Though every now and then I caught him looking at me and suspected I hadn't gone quite to plan.

56

Carol-Ann Jean

It was for a bruise that kept coming up. It kept coming and fading, coming and fading, and then eventually it just sat on my thigh like a piece of bad fruit. Every time I got up in the night and bumped into my dresser, or every time I had to stand and lean across the kitchen table, it hurt me like a pinch.

Miss Ada said some rot had gotten into me and that she'd take it out.

It was my father who came with me and talked to her father in the kitchen.

My father took the day off from the fields even though I told him I could drive there on my own, but he said no. No no no.

Said Miss Ada was a gentle enough sort but her father wasn't quite right. Said her father had a lot of animal in him. Said one time my grandfather was out in the woods and saw Ada's father naked and on all fours, hunting in the brush.

If he was quick to bicker it was because he'd been with Olivia, and she'd said or done something to rub him the wrong way.

—Is she much older than you?

He shook his head. Water ran out his hair and landed on his shoulders.

—How many years?

—Three.

I splashed the river onto my arms. Thought about ducking my head.

—What?

—It's some hold she has on you, is all.

Looking into the sun and scrunching his face against it.

—Don't think I don't know it.

He dove under. Came up again.

—I let too much slide when we were young.

The water caught the light more where he was standing.

—I kept thinking things would be different. Once I got to be a man.

After Olivia our next Cure was Lilia Gedeo, who arrived with her mother in tow. We sat in the kitchen and Mrs. Gedeo described the spasms that took hold of her daughter, that made her flip and coo like she'd a wind trapped inside.

Miss Gedeo was a frequent Cure, and though a grown woman she always came with her mother.

Once Mrs. Gedeo was gone we took Lilia to the sitting room and opened her on the couch nearest the window where I'd seen to Olivia. We quickly found a growth. It had latched onto her rib cage, where its roots had unspooled, thin as thread—partly mucus, partly bone. Saliva cradled in her mouth, as will sometimes happen with a Cure. I emptied it with a small tin cup, pressing its side down on her tongue and gently scooping. Careful not to scrape at the skin of her throat.

Now Father wrapped his hand around the growth and gripped it, sending small cracks throughout the ribs. Those few thin bones would take the longest to heal and so I knew he was still feeling some anger toward me, that he hadn't asked me to reach inside her and save them the trouble of breaking.

He'd been humming for some time.

I emptied the tin cup into the bowl where he hoped to aim the growth, my ears twitching a little, anticipating the splash, and Miss Gedeo lay so still the bubbles in her spit slid around unbroken.

Father liked Miss Gedeo, I knew, because she was quiet and relenting, but it bothered me—how readily her body gave way. No wonder she was so often poorly, giving up of herself so easily. She'd worn herself down. Worn herself thin as an old sheet.

A splash: the bowl shook on the table and Father let out his breath. Over the rim I could see a fragment of the growth. It looked how I imagined pieces of coral looked when they came out of the sea.

—Well?

—Some of it.

He made a displeased, grunting sound.

—Let's put her to ground.

Which we had to do, to make sure the toxins left her—and to heal the ribs.

We started to close her, pulling on the skin that was surprisingly dense for a woman so hardly there.

It was still raining. The lawn made a belching sound. I jumped a little, looked at Father.

—It's just the rain.

—Been a time since I heard it belch.

He didn't reply. Miss Gedeo was on the ground and he was clearing the hair from her eyes.

—Something might have fallen in.

By which he meant an animal. A fox or a hare.

We put her at a fair distance from Mr. Kault, who was still kicking on occasion, and I made sure that her head was to one side and that her lips were only slightly parted. It was hard to arrange her properly with the wet ground spilling in, and so I had to squat in the grave beside her. The rain ran down my shoulders and back like quick, cool fingers and made me wonder if this was what Cures felt when we checked them over.

By the time we'd patted the earth down smooth, evening had settled fully in a mist-blue haze.

Back inside the quiet house I realized how loud the outside air had been.

We spoke briefly of things to be done the next day, and then Father took his coffee to the long couch, smacking his mouth at the tang it put there. I watched him settle back on the cushions, the muscles in his neck releasing, and went to bed.

Father must've been catching some scent on me, some difference I hadn't accounted for. How else could he have known? No one knew about me and Samson. We'd both been careful, knowing how certain Cures would chafe at our being together.

Some would have wanted me burned at the stake, had they known. Others would have been jealous, thinking I was giving him some sort of elixir by lying with him—that he was getting a private, more effective kind of curing. Father had always said

We give them any cause to get frightened and they'll forget how much they need us. Like that. Overnight. They'll want us gone.

The next time I went to meet Samson I thought Father might pester me, but he didn't.

He was chopping in the kitchen and I waited a moment, closing the front door behind me, to see if he'd call, but all I heard was the knife striking the counter.

Samson was at the usual place and we were quiet on the drive to the river. Neither of us mentioned his sister. Outside the truck we stood close to one another and I felt his body warm beside me. I took him inside and felt him move against that sweet bruise he was so good at finding, the two of us rocking until I birthed what felt like a slick, endless pool.

Afterward his breath got so slow I thought he was sleeping. But then,

—How long have we been spending time together?

—Ha! Spending time!

He was lying on his stomach in the grass by the riverbed. My dress was hiked up around my waist and my thighs were itching from the prickling weeds.

—Maybe four months?

—That all?

His voice was thick. Dreams creeping in.

—Feels like longer.

—Does it?

I lay back and fanned my stomach with my dress but it was wet from his sweat and sagged at the hem. I said

—Must be the sneaking around. Makes time go slow.

His face inside the cross of his arms. Eyes closed.

—We could always go somewhere that doesn't need sneaking.

—Sure, but the drive getting there . . . be half a day.

—No.

Flipping onto his back.

—No. I mean the two of us move somewhere. Live somewhere else.

The sky was entirely smooth. Cloudless in a false kind of way.

—You know I can't leave.

—He'd get over it in time.

I let my knees fall together. The wet between my legs had yet to dry.

—We're not Cures.

63

—So?

—We don't work the same way. He wouldn't *get over it*.

—I think you could do it if you wanted to.

I clicked my tongue and sat up, stood up. Looked to the river: thick and still.

—I'm going swimming.

I stepped over him and felt his fingers on my ankle, on the bulge of bone. I took off my dress and dipped it in the water, hung it over a bush to dry, waded in, and looked over my shoulder. He was back on his stomach, his face turned away.

When we first started meeting he'd ask me

—What do you do for fun?

And I'd laugh and say

—Never you mind.

But what I was really thinking was *Nothing. Not a thing aside from this.*

Later, he asked questions like

—What happened when you were born?

—I wasn't born.

—Fine—when you came out the ground.

—Father carried me to the attic and nursed me.

—What did you eat?

—You don't want to know.

—All right. How'd you learn to speak?

—Same as you. Father just spoke to me all the time and soon I'd words of my own.

Only much, much sooner than an infant Cure.

—Why the attic? Seems lonely.

—Because it gets no light, and when I came up my skin still hadn't quite set. Burned easy.

Laughing on his side, on the bedding of our soiled clothes.

—All grown up now, though.

Pinching my arm, squinting and smiling.

—Tough-tough-tough.

When I was a child and Father grew tired of talking the days seemed like they'd go on and on.

—Can't I have a brother?

—No.

—A sister?

—No.

—Why not?

—When you're older you'll have your own child. My time parenting is done.

And so I climbed the trees and hurt the birds, not knowing it was hurt at the time.

I stood on the lawn and watched the twitching progress of a long black feather, its edges uneven and prickling.

Tousled and singed, it lay in the middle of the grass. I wondered if a raven had gotten caught in a chimney.

Father's footsteps sounded from the patio and the feather tumbled away, awkwardly falling over itself back toward the trees.

A rough wind was coming.

I pressed my palms on my thighs to keep my dress down.

Father was standing on The Burial Patch with his shovel—
we were there to bring up Mr. Kault. It was still a little cool,
being so early in the morning, and the grass kept close its dew.

The Ground gave way softly to the shovel, and the soft
gush sound blended with Mr. Kault's middle-born son coming
up the driveway twenty minutes early. After a foot's worth
of digging Father shimmied The Ground aside. We saw his
cheekbones first, then his nose, and then the front-door width
of his chest.

Father got down on his knees to clear away the last bit of
earth, scooping it around the sides of Mr. Kault's panted legs
and sleeved arms. He squatted then and said

—Kault . . . Kault, you can wake up.

Out came his pupils, a pair of deep wet holes, and the irises
surrounding them swirling and brown. His hands grasped at
the low walls of his soil-bed.

He didn't see me as he blinked his way around the
garden—or what he could see of it—and Father asked him
how he was feeling.

There was no need for me to be there aside from the
usual caution—a Cure resisting being aboveground—but
Mr. Kault was fine. I went into the sitting room and sat in
the window while Mr. Kault got changed in the downstairs
bathroom at the far end of the pantry. I'd left his things there.
They'd smelled like outside.

He spent a few minutes drinking water at the kitchen table
while I watched his son kick dust around the drive. The scuffing noise he made seemed timed with the rise and fall of his
father's questions in the kitchen. He was being told we'd
eased the symptoms but that they came from a problem rooted

somewhere we couldn't go. I tried hard not to hear the quiet space Mr. Kault made around himself. Eventually, he said

—How long, then? How long have I got?

Once in the drive Mr. Kault's son grasped him by the arms. The son still had that jittering way of the very young and very strong, and hadn't just then the presence of mind to note the slow horror of his father's gait, the sad shape he made as he swung his bag into the truck.

Father had turned melancholy in the kitchen. I asked if he'd found Mr. Kault to be a tiring Cure. He looked at his hands and said

—What is it you like about him, Ada?

For a moment I thought he meant Mr. Kault and almost said *His broad shoulders, so like your own.* But I caught myself. I went to the pot on the stove and stirred it. There was little point in fighting him. If he knew, he knew.

—Only the feeling he makes inside me.

—It's the Wyde boy? Yes?

Stirring the pot. Squinting through the steam.

—How'd you know it was him?

—He only came by a few months ago. And it's not like you've much choice.

—Fine. I see him every so often and it pleases me.

He sat rock still. I felt him there. Unmoving.

—There's something not right about that boy.

The steam beaded my chest. Turning back to fragrant water.

—Ada.

—What?

—I said you know he's not right.

—Because he likes my company?

—I smelled it on him. Soon as he came into the house.

I dropped the spoon. Let the handle slide too low into the pot.

—I've work to do.

Mr. Sharpe

My wife loves Miss Ada like she's kin but I'm not so sure.
Says she saved our Tabatha, but God forgive me, when our
daughter started speaking she said the strangest things.

    I'm a hare tripping over its too-large feet.

    I'm a caterpillar dropped from a great height.

    They were some of the *first things* to come out her mouth.

    I'm ashamed for thinking it, used to make myself cry with
thinking it, but maybe we weren't meant to have her.

    All water is blood to her. Can you imagine that?

    Your life filled with that much blood?

Upstairs, scrubbing our linens in the bath. The day steaming outside and an ache in my back. Trying to think straight through my anger with Father, wondering how I could distract him or trick him into leaving me be.

And then a truck in the drive. I dropped the wet cloth and the dirty water splashed up at me.

We'd no Cures coming, and nobody ever called around unannounced.

My feet felt bruised on the stairs. I could hear Father coming in from the patio.

I went to the front door.

Mrs. Claudette was landing on her feet with an effort, dropping the keys into her pocket. She called to me

—Hi, Miss Ada.

I would have helped her up the steps, but there was a strangeness to her being there, and she looked tight around the eyes. Pulling herself up one step at a time, one hand on her stomach, breathing hard through her smile.

—I'm sorry for just arriving, but I'm awful worried about the baby.

Some Cures give off a scent when they're lying. The glands get excited and make a liquid akin to sweat. Still, I told her to come inside.

She'd gotten a lot bigger since I'd last seen her. Her feet had learned to bend into little canoes that she rocked the

71

length of with every step, struggling to balance under her own weight.

Father came out of the kitchen. He gazed hard at her midriff, that portion of her body that was doubly alive.

—Best take Mrs. Claudette upstairs.

—Which room?

—The second.

I heard the swish of her fluids as she followed me up the stairs, pulling on the banister. Loud wet puffing sound. Her laugh, once dancing breath, had grit to it now.

—I certainly have gotten bigger—I didn't think that could happen. Lying on my back I can barely breathe.

—It'll all ease quickly, soon as it's born.

Your little green-eyed boy.

In the bedroom I lifted her feet onto the bed and leaned over her, moving the pillows behind her head.

Into my chest she said

—Your father, is he—

—He doesn't like unscheduled Cures. Tell me why you're worried.

—I'd some blood this morning. And my stomach hasn't been right.

—All right, I'll look inside.

She nodded and watched me, her face tight.

She reached out a hand and put it on mine. Her skin was as Samson's would have been, had he not been those years in the field.

—Miss Ada, what happens when you have a baby with someone you're not supposed to?

—Don't fret, Mrs. Claudette. I've never seen adultery get into a baby.

The words fell out of me. She was twisting the front of her dress. She looked up at me, her lashes velvety and thick.

—Is there anything that *can* get in?

—. . . You mean like shock?

—No, I mean like other things you're not supposed to do.

Her shoulders were prickling in the cool shade of the bedroom, their little hairs awoken.

—From here everything seems fine, but let me look inside.

She lay back and closed her eyes, the thin lids crinkling. I put her to sleep and pulled up her dress. Her belly had grown a thick pink line from button to groin. I pulled down her panties and looked at the stain inside the frilled cotton cloth: quick, bright tendril of pink. She split open like a barrel, the skin hard and unfolding. I saw the outline of the child, saw him kick at the gust of air come to meet him.

I looked down and saw a little growth—most likely a remnant of her previous curing—that was causing her to leak but doing no harm besides. It clung like a berry to the side of her womb. Placing my hand over it I hummed a tune and within a few moments it had gone away with a popping sound.

When I woke her I told her everything was fine, but that she shouldn't spend so much time on her feet. She nodded and gazed up at me, sinking her pretty white teeth into her pretty pink lip.

She's not listening to me at all, only watching.

—Is there anything else, Olivia?

The muscles 'round her mouth working into a soft pout.

Must be a trick of hers, to put the men in mind of kissing.

—Well, yes. I'm worried about my brother, Miss Ada.

She squirmed inside her dress. I felt my voice jump in my throat, but when I spoke I made sure I sounded easy and light.

—Why? Is he poorly?

—He's sick. He's not right.

She looked down at her hands and folded them.

—Tell him to come for a curing.

—I don't think it's something that can be fixed, Miss Ada.

—Then why are you telling me about it?

She flinched, as though I'd pinched her. I'd liked to have slapped her creamy cheek, to stop her from speaking, with Father downstairs.

—I just need to know if my baby is a girl.

—. . . You're not worried about jinxes?

—I need to know if the baby will be safe around Samson.

Like a warm bath, she slid into her lies.

—I don't follow.

—When it's growing up . . . if it's a girl, and if we're living with Samson . . . I won't be leaving them alone.

And then she looked at me through her lashes. Bud of a mouth a little bit open. Her dark hair fell into her eyes and she left it there.

That won't work, I wanted to tell her. *That won't work on me.*

Father made no noise downstairs.

—It's a boy.

She didn't gasp or sigh or make any of the relieved noises that Cures make. Her voice was flat and hard.

—You're sure?

—Certain.

She kept looking at me and I kept looking at her, and then, slowly, she pushed her lips together again.

—Well then, that makes things easier.

And she was sitting up without any assistance from me.

I helped her down the stairs and out to the car. I didn't know where Father had gone, how much he had heard.

—Miss Ada, can I pay you next week?

—Don't worry about paying me this time. There really was very little to do.

By now she was twisting the keys in their particular way that saw the truck spurred to life once more.

—Oh, thank you, Ada. Thank you.

All the concern gone from her now. Looking at me like she might laugh or wink, her shoulders sliding down her back, readying herself to preen in the breeze.

—Us girls must stick together.

I went back inside and called into the kitchen, told Father I was tired and going to bed. He made a "Hmph" sound that I barely heard with thinking all the things I'd liked to have said.

I'd be not right too, with a sister like you.

The next day I'd planned on meeting Samson.

I didn't know if I'd tell him what Olivia had said, if he'd know why she said it. I'd never known a Cure to speak of a sibling—of any blood relation—in such a way. Of course there was something different about him: he wasn't afraid of me—of being taken inside me. Didn't care about the ways I was unlike Cure women. But why would Olivia claim he'd hurt a child?

Like I said, I'd planned on seeing him, but that morning I opened my eyes to a weak, faltering sound—some small thing crying and the mewl of it waking me. Slow and dazed I followed the weepy noise into the kitchen, climbing onto the counters and looking into the bowl we kept atop the cupboard. Wide enamel bowl with its blue rim, and inside of it a baby. Or rather, the outline of a baby. Only a whisper of a thing, neatly swaddled in the blanket we kept there.

I went to the back door and called to Father. I told him within half an hour we'd have a startled and panicking Cure. He was digging and didn't turn around.

I went upstairs and put on a large black shirt that wouldn't show up stains. It had a wide pocket on its front, and I went down to the bottom of the garden and filled it with sorrel leaves, stuffing it as though it was my own animal pouch.

Sooner than I'd thought, I heard screen-door-slam.

I walked into the house and already the couple was on the stairs. Father turned to me and said their name—Bennett-Kent. In the second spare room Father eased Mrs. Bennett-Kent back onto the pillows while her husband removed her feet from their thin-soled shoes. I was pulling on the leaves in my pocket, making them limp, easier to chew. How different Mrs. Bennett-Kent was to Olivia. Both large with child, both with dark hair that snaked over the pillows, but different all the same.

—Ada will see to you.

Mr. Bennett-Kent was not a well-proportioned man; his hands were too large for his arms and the calluses across his knuckles made them seem larger still. Mrs. Bennett-Kent had large black eyes that followed her husband out of the room.

—Are you in pain?

She nodded, her lips pursing, and said

—I've a tightness in my stomach, like a spasm.

—I'm going to take a look inside you. Close your eyes.

She closed up her face so quietly I thought *She must have been told good things*.

I peeled back the wet slap of her womb. The baby was still in evidence, like the unevenness to grass where some animal has stopped to graze. Its shadow-outline turned away from me and I knew its other half did the same in the bowl downstairs. A sound came from her, the deepening lilt at the end of a song, and I picked up the rhythm of a slow healthy pulse.

The spasm that riddled her had started the night before and was working to spoil her lining, had left the baby with nothing to eat, so I took out the mulchen leaves and placed the new bedding inside of her womb.

The leaves settled around the curve of the baby's back until the lining was plush and wet again. I sang faster, a jumping tune that picked up the pace of the baby's heart and put suckle back in its cord. After a time the little body got denser. I didn't know what had caused the spasm. All of her seemed healthy now, and calm.

First thing she did when I woke her was put a hand to her mouth.

—That taste—it's like I've been sucking on a penny.

I told her what I'd seen and asked her if she'd gotten a fright the day before. I put out my hands for her to take hold of and, as she sat upright, watched the flesh of her thighs pool out beneath her.

Her skin, deeply brown, was glowing a little now.

—Well, yes, last night . . . but there was no harm in it.

She told me that the night before she'd been up much later than usual. With her husband lost to some unforeseen task in the fields she'd closed the house up *extra tight*, and close to midnight she checked, for maybe the fourth time, the lock on the screen door. She rattled the door in its peeling wooden frame the way an intruder might.

—To make sure it wouldn't give, you see.

She'd leaned on the wall, letting the weight of her belly settle.

—. . . Because my back is so sore these days, so tender—

But then she jumped, because she could see the shape of a person outside, someone standing in the yard and gazing toward her.

In the dark she made out the shape of them, thicker than the rest of the night.

—You could just tell it was a person, alive.

Standing as if waiting to cross the street.

And then she turned off the light, and with the kitchen and garden in equal dark she saw that not only, yes, there *was* a person, but that somehow, in these few moments, this person was now come very close to the house. Was, in fact, standing on the patio step with only the slim parting of the screen door keeping them out of the house.

—I didn't scream, exactly, but I tell you, Miss Ada, I jolted like a horse, and then realized it was only Lorraine! My good friend Lorraine Languid. Well, we stood there laughing

for I don't know how long before I thought to turn on the
light.

So much talk for so nonsense a story.

I started tugging the duvet back into place, letting her
know it was time to leave. I scolded myself, for getting
worked up over the baby, and for letting a Cure take up so
much time.

—It's normal to get a shock seeing someone in your garden that late at night.

—Well, yes, Miss Ada, and I said to Lorraine I never
mind her coming over but it's a strange way to announce
oneself, standing in the garden—and what would she have
done if I hadn't seen her? And gone to bed and locked her
out for the night?

I was tugging her skirt down toward her ankles, bothered
by the shuffling sound it made around her knees.

I thought of the Lorraine I'd met as a child. Lorraine and
her lambs and her smoking mouth.

—She would have gone home, soon enough.

Mrs. Bennett-Kent looked at me, her large breasts pulling
at the buttons of her shirt.

*There's more to this fright. Of course there's more, if it was
strong enough to spoil her baby's bedding.*

—Oh no, Miss Ada, you're thinking of the old granite
houses on the right side of town. We live on the *left* side.

—Yes, that's right—

—Our gardens don't all back onto the same little lane.

I often forgot, as it was rarely relevant, that there were
two types of houses in town, and that most Cures felt it a kind
of distinction to live on the left side.

—I see, I—

—On the *left* side we each have our own private yard, though of course they're small, but you can leave children out back and let them play, because you see they can't go anywhere.

—Yes, of course. I see what you mean.

For I did see now, though she was eager to keep speaking and the words came breathless and fast.

—And well, Miss Ada, I haven't been in the fields of late. With the birth so close, I've been staying at home, and for all of yesterday I was busying myself in the garden, and then at about five I came in for my bath and . . . and, well, the thing is, Miss Ada, I've always been fond of Lorraine but she's not above acting strange and I don't know exactly how long she was wandering around my damn house.

She moved the hair out of her face and made to laugh. As if the laugh would undo the venom.

—Strange behavior, I said. Strange behavior, to be sure.

When they had left I went into the kitchen to make certain the bowl was empty, and it was, though the blanket still held a soft smell of orchids, of milk freshly churned.

I rarely wore black on account of the heat, and when I saw myself in the mirror I startled. I looked like my own shadow-twin. I went into my room to change and noticed that the ivy was growing thickly through my open window, latching onto the already chipping paint. The whole of the house was warm and creaking. I opened my wardrobe and pulled on the first thing I saw, leaving the shirt in a dark pool on the floor.

—You're going to meet him?

I turned around with the smock snagging around my neck and shoulders.

—I'm going out for a walk.

—Ada, he's not safe.

—For who? Cure girls and women?

—His own sister—

—Is a snake if I ever saw one.

—His own sister doesn't want him around girls—

—And what's that got to do with me?

He was quiet then. The old tension between us, that he'd made me in this halted way.

—It doesn't worry you?

—When did we start worrying over things without being paid to?

—So you don't care that he's sick. That it's his sickness that makes him want you.

—You're going off rumors.

—You know what you look like to them.

—What does it matter? He won't hurt me.

—Won't *try* to hurt *you*.

—Right.

—Because he knows he *can't*.

A few moments' quiet. I pulled the smock down over my chest.

—You're letting that sickness grow inside him.

—Even if that's true, it's not the kind of sick we're concerned with.

—Sick is sick is sick. It's got to go somewhere.

—This sickness is not my problem.

—No! Only your pleasure. Till you're no longer enough and it's some Cure girl he climbs on top of.

—That happens, it's his fault, not mine. And what do you want me to do? Kill him? Castrate him?

—I only know I don't want you lying with him.

—Father—

—I'm telling you not to lie with him.

I bit hard on my lip and walked by him, the soft skin on his arm grazing mine.

—I think some of his sick has gotten inside you.

—You think what you want. No one's stopping you.

Concord Jackson

Miss Ada was our resident fairy. Magicking everyone's sickness away.

Are you sick? Is that why you're looking for her?

When I got to the truck it was still wavy with heat, so he couldn't have been there long.

—You're late, I said.

—So are you.

He ran a hand under his cap, into his short soft hair.

—We go to the river?

I nodded and opened the passenger door. The handle was hot in my hand and the worn leather hot on my legs. We drove with the windows down and I leaned out, letting my hair whip.

When we got to the river he opened the door but before he put his legs out I said

—So I've seen your sister twice now.

He didn't look at me but rested back in the seat again.

—What she want?

—For me to look at the baby. What else would there be?

—The baby all right?

—The baby is fine.

—Is she all right?

There was a sneer in his voice, a venom he didn't think I'd catch.

—She is, aside from worries about her brother.

His arms were loose in his lap. He looked straight out the window now, into the trees where shade was waiting. I couldn't let on I didn't believe her if I wanted him to tell me about the strangeness between them.

—You really think I'm a bad man, Ada?

—I think your own sister's afraid of you.

—Don't . . . don't let Olivia fool you.

—And why would she be out to fool me, Samson? What is it you don't want to tell me?

—So Olivia comes around telling stories and I have to make excuses.

—She says you're sick and that she's worried you'll hurt the baby.

—Me!

Laughing and his hard eyes dancing. He got out of the truck, quickly, and I followed him. The grass cracked under my feet. The river was loud and I couldn't hear what he said as he walked away from me.

—Samson!

He turned and his eyes were pink at their corners.

—Anything happens to that baby it's Olivia. Soon as it's out of her she's liable to eat it with a spoon.

—Why would she say all this? Is she that bad a person?

—Says I'm sick. She's the sick one.

—Sick like how?

He looked in the river. Spat.

—You've seen inside her.

—All I saw was a baby.

Shifting his belt. Wanting to take it off; the hot metal chafing him.

—Sick like how, Samson?

—She's just not right.

And now he was taking off his clothes and walking into the river he'd spat in.

—You can't be specific?

—'S hard. She's been this way a long time.

—Since when?

—Since we were young.

—Before you were orphaned?

—No.

—After, then.

He looked up, into the trees. The water waist-deep. I stayed where I was though the long grass was itching me.

—So what happened?

He was clenching his cheeks like he wanted his gums to start bleeding.

—After our parents died we moved in with Auntie, but we were always cooped up and alone. And she'd never had kids, didn't know what to do with us. We'd a half deck of cards we used to play with.

—And . . . Olivia turned at some stage?

—When I was ten and she was thirteen.

I chewed on my cheek, said

—Girls mature faster.

Girl Cures, with their secrets and their sideways glances.

—Indeed they do.

—Could you have told your aunt?

—Auntie was already old. No match for Olivia.

He was up to his chest. Kept splashing his face to cover his tears.

—When she moved in with Harry I thought it was all done with. But then they couldn't get along.

87

I looked to the reeds and saw his vest snagged there. It had caught at an angle that made it look like a wisp of smoke, thin and pale.

—Once she made me sit outside all night and there was ice 'tween my toes in the morning.

I came in the front door, itching and irritable with the feel of the hot day sticking to me. The whole walk home a phantom Olivia was strutting beside me, singing and shaking out her hair.

Inside the hall I took one step, then another. Moved hushed as I could as I made for the stairs. Still, he heard me; said my name and told me to come into the kitchen. He was sitting at the table and his chest was glowing. Full of heat. His shirt uneven across his shoulders with a look of fur bristling.

—We need to redirect some roots. They're coming too close to the house.

I looked out the window, to the tall silent trees.

—And what? They're gonna come up through the floor?

He was holding a mug and kept looking inside it, thinking he'd magic it full of coffee again.

—No. But they'll grow criss and cross. Make it harder to put Cures in The Ground.

Garden work was the last thing I felt like, but I couldn't say no. Not when I'd been away from the house all day. Not when anything at all might give him cause to talk about Samson.

How Samson stopped me doing my share.

How Samson made me lazy, how Samson made me slow.

We went out back and the dry crackle in the air felt stronger there than it had at the river.

If I put The Ground in my mouth it'd be spicy, rich.

We walked toward the end of the garden, straight over the grass as the weather had baked shut the dangerous soil.

The trees seemed to give off their own separate heat. The closer we came to them the more it felt like a hand on the back of my neck. The hedged growth around them, brittle and thick with briar. A few more weeks and roses would start to grow there.

—Here.

Father parting the growth, making not quite enough space for me to pass through.

—Go through and tell me where you see the roots are risen.

I looked at the thickety branches, the tangle of stem.

—Go through there, I said.

—Yes, he said, not catching my tone. Go through here and see where the roots are risen.

—And then what?

—And then what do you think? We'll sing to them. I'll pass you the song.

Which meant he'd sing it to me, chord by chord, and I'd keep on repeating him until the work was done. I pulled my dress up around my waist and took a sideways step. A thin branch swung back and scraped my knee.

—Be a little swift, Ada.

I'd a pain in my jaw and realized it was my teeth, grinding. I thought of Samson's hard cheeks, his child body hurting with cold.

Another step, another scrape, another step. A thorn in my left heel.

I wanted to wipe a cloth over my face and lie down in the cool of my room.

—Can you see anything?

—Not yet.

Being careful not to snap. Careful not to bicker. Nothing about me unusual, nothing calling for conversation or attention. Inside of the hedge now and squatting down to part it a little further, ready to call back to him that I could see no troublesome growth, only brittle ground.

But then I *was* seeing something.

A pile of waste that had no cause to be there.

Pale branches, mostly yellowish and thin. Or rather, they would have been branches, but their color and shape weren't right. Where had they come from? From some strange tree since extinct in our garden? But there were so many of them, it made no sense that they'd all tumbled at once, in this close spot, and then stayed here.

I reached for the closest one, long and thick, and once I had it in my hand I felt a sadness seep into me. A puffing, breathy kind of sadness that a Cure might feel right after they finished crying.

Father said my name in such a way I knew it wasn't the first time.

—What are these?

What I wanted to say: *What are these, and why are they crying?*

I held the would-be branch above my head and looked up over my shoulder, could see only part of him—he'd crescented his arm to push the prickle-growth further aside, but otherwise he wasn't moving.

—I'd forgotten they were here.

I turned around fully then, though my legs were scratching pinker and pinker and my dress getting torn besides. Snagged in a swirl around me. He was looking at it in my hand but making no move to touch it.

It was high afternoon now and the sun was an upturned bucket above us. I didn't like the color this branch turned when the light came through.

—What are they?

His nose moved a half inch up his face, came down again.

—Your predecessors.

I knew what he meant. Right away I knew, but my thoughts kept darting around. I said

—They're branches.

On one side of the branch I could see an indentation. A divot. Very smooth.

—That's the problem. They should be bones.

And now he did move to touch it, taking it from me and moving his forearm slowly past my cheek.

—You can see—here . . .

He twisted its other side toward me.

—You can see here where it started to turn . . .

A bird in a tree, trilling. I thought *If I ask him to stop talking he will.*

—This happened a few times. They'd take on the color or the shape or the density in places, and then they'd stop, and then nothing I could do would get them going again.

He tossed it back onto the pile. It made a tinny, echoey sound when it landed.

—Can you see the roots?

—But there's so many.

—Where?

—Not roots. So many of these.

—You knew you weren't my only try.

—Yes, but . . .

I wanted to say *It's not how I was made that bothers me, or that it took you so long to get it right. It's that you left these here, not caring that I might find them. It's that you tossed these half-formed things away without ceremony. That you wouldn't pretend, even in these few moments, that any of it was special to you at all.*

What I knew he'd say in return:

Sounds like a Cure's gotten under your skin, Ada.

He was looking around for the roots again. Every time he moved he blocked a different side of the sun.

—Nothing sacred about birth, Ada. You know that. No matter the species.

—I know.

—Unspectacular business, coming into the world.

—Yes. I know.

These felled versions of myself. What about them could not cohere? What about them went wrong that the earth wouldn't compact into organ or the branches blanch into bone?

—How many are there?

—How many tries? Including you?

I had a pain in my heart and put a hand there, heard myself make an angry bark of a sound, thinking *heart* was the wrong word to use.

—Ada.

—Yes.

—You know how you were made.

—Yes.

—You've always known.

—Yes.

—Help me find these roots.

I moved around on my knees, finding the risen roots and spending an hour singing them backward and down. Back into The Ground, back the way they came.

That night I dreamt of my partial siblings. Dreamt myself crouching beside them and asking if they could hear me. Dreamt them angry at me for coming together, for walking around whole and entire.

What's so special about you, Ada? Why do you get to be alive?

But I wasn't born alive, I told them. *I've only been alive a little while.*

Meaning only since I met Samson, and then the branch-bones laughed at me. And well they might. It was a foolish thing to say, even in a dream. Foolish to fall in line with a Cure's girlhood and imagine such feelings belonged to me. But I *had* been living a muted kind of life, and I had gone all this time without meeting someone who'd fall asleep, of their own accord, beside me.

Paula Greene

Go visit her now?
    Oh, I think it'd be too much for me.
    We're all so old now, and she still looks the same . . .
    Besides, she stopped seeing to us after her father died,
and there's no other reasons to go there—you don't exactly
call in for tea.

—She must've liked him enough if she had a baby with him.

—I keep telling you. When Olivia looks at people she doesn't see people. She sees means to ends.

—Why do you put up with her?

—She's my sister. We're orphans. . . . What?

—If Father treated me badly he'd stop being my father.

—Ha! You think he treats you well?

—He does.

—So well you have to sneak around to see me. So well he puts you to work every day.

—It's not work. It's what I was made for.

—Looks a lot like labor—and poorly paid.

He was arguing now for the sake of it, as was his way.

—Well, whatever about anything else, Father is set to do something.

—Like what?

—I don't know. Something to keep us apart.

He looked into the trees. I couldn't see his eyes for the shadowy shade. I said

—We'll leave.

He looked at me. His eyes still a band of black.

—We will?

—Yes.

His face creasing and uncreasing. The quiver in his mouth.

—I need you to come get me at the house tonight, without the truck. Come for me after dark and I'll be ready.

—Without the truck?

—Yes.

—But a storm is coming.

—Father will hear it if you bring the truck.

He took a breath and held it, started nodding.

—All right?

—All right.

I'd a plan that I didn't know would work. I'd had to come up with it so quick. It'd be long, it'd make me weary, it'd cause me some pain and it'd be risky, and it'd all be undone if Father wasn't in the form to hunt because of the storm.

He drove me back up the road. Before I got out of the truck I straightened my dress, said

—Is that why you like being with me?

Looking at me blank.

—Is that why you don't mind being with me the way I am? Not a Cure, and everything else.

—What's everything else? What Olivia's done?

I thought of a small, freckled Samson. I couldn't picture Olivia as a child.

—Dammit, Ada. You think you're so strange. You're not that strange. Strangest thing about you is you don't get sick and tired of everyone complaining at you all the time.

His face as open to me as a book or a flower.

I couldn't help it; started laughing.

Melinda Sacran

I saw her in the woods and she was lying with a wolf.

I was twelve and I ran away from home and I saw her with her arms around the wolf and it was licking her neck.

Licking her like she was sweating gravy.

I ran all the way home again and had a fever for days but I had to hide it because if I was sick I'd be taken to her.

Been hiding and ignoring sicknesses my whole life.

People tried to tell me I was seeing things but I saw her.

I saw her.

I still dream about that long pink tongue and her with her head back. Laughing.

I got back to the house and Father was clucking into The Burial Patch.

He heard me come onto the patio and turned around.

—Going hunting later?

He looked at my wet smock and my mussed hair.

—How was your walk?

There was a bulge in my throat that I hoped didn't show.

—I'll stop seeing him.

He picked up the shovel and wedged it in The Ground.

—Just like that?

—He wouldn't give me any straight answers.

In the sunshine he was glowing. His grey-blond hair looked like a cap of pure light.

—You'll find something else that pleases you.

—I will.

He nodded.

—Well, I'm glad.

I looked at my dusty feet, and when he didn't say anything else I went inside.

About an hour or so later, the storm started. Quiet at first, and then all of a sudden the trees were thrashing and the windows and doors were shaking in their frames. I had to keep relighting the stove.

Once the sun went down, I could see Father itching to go. He draped his shirt and pants over a kitchen chair and started rolling his shoulders, wiggling his jaw. He dropped to all fours and looked back at me, squatted with kindling on my knees. It suited him better, his animal gait. Though his limbs were modeled on a Cure male they were always ready to bend, his shoulders happily slinking forward and his hips rising behind him, the muscles in his legs pulled taut and presenting themselves. I think it was a mistake in his making, but one that suited him. Now in the kitchen he clicked and clucked, his tongue for the moment giving up speech, and I said

—Enjoy, Father. See you in the morning.

The twigs crackled orange when I tossed them in the stove. Made the kitchen tiles look flushed like too-warm cheeks.

An hour or so went by and the storm grew and grew and I was too restless to stay inside. I went out to the porch, and so I saw him when he came. I saw him come out of the trees. Bobbing ball of white, which was his shirt catching the occasional sliver of moonlight. He staggered a little side to side with the wind and his boots heavy with mud. He looked cautiously toward the house and I waved my arms over my head so he could see me through the rain.

He'd a jacket on over his shirt but he'd left the jacket open and it was all wet through.

—Come in for a minute, to dry.

—Your father?

—He's out. We'll be gone before he's back.

If he wondered at Father being out he didn't say. Probably he was too cold to question why I'd lied.

102

I brought him into the kitchen and he went straight to the stove, shivering. The back of his neck shone gold and smooth in the half-light of the stove and I put my mouth there, my hands on his back, high on the balls of my feet. He turned his head a little and I rested my cheek against him.

—You all right?

—I just need to do one thing before we go.

I made for the patio door. He'd cupped his hands to his mouth and looked at me over his braided fingers.

—I want to say goodbye to the garden.

His eyes narrowed a little.

—It's where I played as a child.

And when I put out my hand he took it, and together we went out the back door.

The rain was so loud, the wind so high, that he put his arm up over his face. We walked over The Burial Patch, stopped just short of the lawn with its grass thick and wet.

Jeremy Loan

One thing I do remember, and I feel silly bringing it up.

When I was young and my mother needed her ulcer seen to, we went to the house. Miss Ada and I looked to be 'round the same age then and we went outside and . . . Like I say. Sounds silly. She got me to lie on top of her. I didn't know what she wanted right away, and when I realized I couldn't— she'd nothing there. And . . . her eyes. When she realized. I got up and ran away. I knew by her eyes. She was going to eat me. I thought *If I don't get away she'll eat me. If she can't have me one way she'll have me another.*

When I pushed him, I couldn't tell if he made a sound.

He fell to his knees and looked back at me, his face knotted against the rain. His hands and knees sucked a half inch into The Ground, quickly turned black-brown.

He was irked, confused and cold. There was a quick stir in my chest, which was the urge to help him up. To stop it while I could. The jacket looked like an animal pelt draped over him.

And then The Ground started taking him. It opened just enough to swallow his legs to his waist so he was upright, looking all around him, trying to put his hands down flat, but of course he couldn't take hold.

I could tell it liked the taste of him because it took him so slow.

I hopped onto a stone when he reached for me, and quickly he started reaching for the earth again, trying to pull himself out. Handful of mud after handful of mud, and his face, still so beautiful with the horror run through it.

—I can't leave, and you can't stay. The Ground will keep you safe.

His head back, mouth open. Screaming.

—And we'll be better suited, once you rise.

His eyes going left and right, up and down. His face an almond-colored pool in the black mud, his ears filling.

—She won't find you here. And The Ground will take your hurt away, all the hurt she put inside you.

His curls. Flecked with nutmeg shavings. His cheekbones.
The lips that had been on mine. I squatted, touched his face,
said

—Close your mouth, close your eyes.

When I was a child, up in the trees.

There got to be a time when all the birds knew to stay
away from me.

It's a hard thing to get across, being that kind of alone.

Lydia Bell

No, none of the men went near her.

All sorts of reasons. Rumors, for starters—it'd get bitten off; she'd eat you after. All that nonsense.

But also, you know, she looked *quite young*.

Not like a child, to my mind, but not fully grown.

A young woman, *I'd* have said . . . or getting to be.

Most of us found it sweet, comforting, but a few found it . . . unnerving.

When I woke in the morning, I thought maybe I'd dreamt it all.

Or maybe he'd come for me and I'd slept through.

I went down into the kitchen and saw Father looking out at The Ground, stood safely on a stone.

I opened the patio door and kept it open with my hip, pulled my cardigan around me.

—How were the woods?

He half turned around.

—Loud, he said. Loud and wet.

He hadn't dressed yet and was covered all over with mud.

—Be doubly sure to stay off The Ground today.

When I didn't say anything he looked at me full.

—That storm last night . . . it's wakeful. Stay well clear.

He walked past me and I followed him, watched him wash himself down with a towel and sit at the kitchen table, letting himself dry. I was worried he'd catch some scent off me, some mischief-musk, but he seemed to have taken me at my word. Sitting across from him, the day seemed like any other, only I'd a taste in my mouth that I knew was heartache.

—What time are we bringing up Miss Gedeo?

—You know what time. Eight.

His mug was on the table and I twirled my fingers 'round its rim.

—You've a Cure tomorrow.

I made a lilting, agreeable sound and watched the inside of the mug.

—You remember Lorraine Languid.

—Sure. Fred Languid's widow, Mr. Kault's cousin. Lorraine of the lambs.

He ignored the laugh in my voice.

—The change is on her. She needs it eased.

I thought of Lorraine taking me into the barn and the lambs moving toward her. The womby smell come rich off their wool. I said

—It's been on her a long time already. She must be almost done.

—It doesn't agree with her.

—So . . . I'm to steady it?

He shook his head, standing now.

—Just hurry it along.

Women Cures did ask for this on occasion. The quicker to get back to work. No time for a chorus of rising flushes and leaning against the cool part of the wall. But Lorraine Languid had never worked in the fields.

—Why does she need it hurried, though?

But he was at the stove now, tired of me, tired of chatter.

Dim, blunt sound: the wooden spoon nudging the bottom of the pan.

For weeks afterward, an animal followed me.

It was always next to me, just a little to one side.

An animal with four legs and a cropped tail and a wound

for a mouth. I told myself it was only a heartsick dream, but every time I looked I saw it big and clear and alive.

Eager to dip its muzzle in my open chest.

It wanted to eat my heart and sometimes I wanted to let it; I missed him like he was a limb.

I tried saying his name to myself, thinking I'd find some comfort or soothe in the soft coupling.

Sam-son

Sam-son

Son-Sam

The sound of it quickly lost on me, the hiss of the *s* losing its lull and becoming as meaningless as any other name. And still, on and on the shuffling of the short-tailed creature beside me. His red mouth pointed at my heart.

I'd sit down on the back step, looking at the lawn.

Put a hand on my low-belly.

That place he'd been.

PART III

Bringing up Miss Gedeo was always slow-paced and tentative on account of her weight and size. Father once said she was built like a birdcage, and even her heart struck me as birdlike. A small bird. Watchful and hurried.

I watched Father clear away the earth and remembered the sight of his hand inside her, his fist the size of his own large heart up behind her ribs. The soft cloth of the gown we'd buried her in fell into the dips of her collarbone and crumpled there. Father leaned close and blew the dirt from her eyes.

—Miss Gedeo, you can wake up now.

When she didn't stir I whistled the sound of her name. The wind had a cold bite and I pulled my cardigan tighter around me. We watched her come up to her elbows and smile. She opened her mouth to speak, and then her arms went from under her and her throat rolled upward in a taut, unnatural arc. Her breath was caught there, in the tight of her throat. She couldn't breathe, and her eyes were set to fail her. She reached out for Father, who stood looking down at her, clucking his tongue.

I got on my knees and put my mouth over hers and put a tunnel of breath between us. Her lips tasted of earth and I thought of Samson's mouth, the loam thick on his lips.

Under my hand: her heart going wild.

When I took my mouth away her eyes were quick and watchful.

Father put down his shovel and squatted to give her his hand.

Her lips had tasted of The Ground.

—You all right, Miss Gedeo?

She nodded and looked to her soil-filled lap, wanting to clean it away though the whole of her was covered in dirt, and then she started on in her honeyed way, talking about how much better she felt, how *well*.

Back inside she changed in the downstairs toilet, and from the pantry I heard her sighing and contentedly folding up her gown. A fresh one fell around her legs, the rush of its hem sounding like her own name drawn long at its narrowest points.

Liiliia.

Listening to her I wondered if maybe she had a fondness for The Ground, for the fact of our hands having been inside of her.

She opened the bathroom door and I went quickly into the kitchen.

—Thank you again, Miss Ada. I feel I could almost run.

—Not to worry Miss Gedeo, you're hardly any work at all.

—I always feel so clean and right, after you've been inside me.

And then she laughed a little at herself, at the strangeness of her phrasing. Though her new dress was clean, her face and throat and arms were still colored grey from being underground.

—I mean, I always know once you've looked inside that everything's as it should be.

I smiled at her and leaned back on the counter, wanting her to leave.

—It was Father that tended to you, mostly.

Her hands were at her chest and she squeezed them together now. In a flat voice she said

—Oh, is that right.

—That's why your ribs are a touch cracked. Because there wasn't enough room in you. For his hands.

A watery sheen came over her eyes.

—I . . . thought I remembered your mouth on me.

—You'd lost a little breath, so I gave you some of mine.

Squeezing and squeezing her small white hands.

—I see.

She started looking around the room, looking at the walls in the lightbulb light.

—It's just, there was such a softness to it.

—To which?

—Your mouth.

And then the sound of her mother in the drive outside. She stopped holding her hands and started holding her shoulders, rubbing her arms up and down.

—Miss Gedeo, you ever feel unwell, you come here. Don't come here besides.

She turned away and picked up her bag and I knew she was crying.

Father had come in. He looked at Miss Gedeo, looked at me, and I shrugged: *Cures*. I made myself some tea while he took her outside, and avoided my face in the black of the kitchen window.

Mrs. Delilah Sharpe

Of course I remember it.

Cruel hot day.

I called Will into the kitchen and he looked at my legs but I wouldn't look down. I could feel it and that was enough for me. He took me out to the truck and we didn't say a word because where else would he be taking me?

Not that we've a name for him.

When I was a child we called him Mr. Fix.

We got to the house and I still wouldn't look, though by then I could smell it. The mean metal smell. I don't remember getting into the house, just the rocking chair. That damn chair tilting to and fro with him knelt beside me and peering between my legs. I remember he told me not to move and I wanted to say *I'm not moving, it's this damn chair you've made me sit in* but I thought if I spoke it'd put more strain on the baby.

How long we were there I don't know. Him ripping up sheet after sheet and trying to stanch the flow and singing—the whole time he kept on singing—and then he looked up and told me again not to move and then his daughter was in the room.

Little Miss Ada.

And she'd a bundle in her arms.

A red-streaked barely moving bundle of cloth. And then she said what she said and I thought *My baby, that's my baby*, and Will was crying and I thought *I should hold his hand*.

121

When we came home the blood was still on the floor, and even then, through the happiness, I thought *What a sight this would be if our baby had died*. But she didn't die. No matter what's wrong with her. My beautiful girl.

I'll not have an ill word said against Miss Ada.

It was close to two when Lorraine arrived.

From my window I watched the car approach while the rain spat and settled in a mist above the grass. Whoever drove her to the bottom of the drive looked away as she made for the house, drove away without helping her with her bag, which was clearly heavy.

She didn't seem to mind.

She walked like a woman who'd grown up slim.

The small heel of her shoes saw her wobble once or twice, one arm stretched away from her body and the other pulled taut by the weight of the bag. When she came closer I could smell it: cigarettes and cold cream and the foil that Cure candies come wrapped in.

The thin fabric of her dress moved over her hips and thighs with the same frenzy of a lightbulb flickering before it finally expires, and the scoop of her armpits had the velvety look of charcoal after a fire.

Hot, hot weather. It took its toll on older bodies.

I went to the door and I opened it and right away she pointed at her bag and said her lower back was tender. I took the drooping handles in my hand, felt the moist fingerly grooves.

Inside the hall she leaned back to look at me.

—Why, Ada, I do believe you've grown.

The most I could have grown was a half inch or so. I suppose she said it because it's something Cure children and adolescents like hearing.

I left her bag behind the sitting room door and told her she might sit for a moment. Her freckles gathered close about her lips, a sign she'd soon be smiling.

Upstairs Father was standing in his bedroom, his back to the door.

—Just open her in the sitting room.

—You'll not be coming down?

—You know your way.

—And you don't want to talk to her?

—No.

He'd left a towel hanging over the chair. I picked it up and held it in both hands.

—This feels very strange to me. Curing her without your coming down. Without talking to her at all.

—You're getting older now. You don't need me watching over you all the time.

I helped Lorraine lift her stocking feet onto the couch and asked her to leave her hands at her sides. If she wondered after Father she didn't say. Her dress was lined with buttons down its front, and once I'd laid my hand across her eyes and seen her sleeping I undid them one by one.

I looked at her belly, at the belts of fat falling under their own slack weight and pooling 'round her waist.

She smelled like a rag left near the sink. I peeled away her underthings and wedged the towel up between her legs and a little ways underneath her. My thumb, when I ran it along the soft inside of her arm, saw the blood come heavy and slow. This we did with women past a certain age, relieve some of the pressure that gets into their blood. But her blood was extra thick. So thick I half expected the opened vein would shimmy up flecks of iron, as pebble-bedded streams will sometimes in a certain light reveal shards and lumps of gold.

After a few moments I pushed the skin back together and wiped it clean with my dress. The skin of her stomach fell easily apart, its elastic long gone. The ovaries were all sinewy and very small, lined with the deep grooves of a peach stone, and her womb shone with an unseemly wet.

It made me think of staling fruit that takes on the shape of the bowl it sits in.

I held a hand over it, felt its heat. I wondered it didn't turn the flesh of her stomach pink. I ran a finger down its middle and it opened slack and uneven as her sleeping mouth. Inside was the usual liquid, only cordial-thick.

I sang the sound of water in a drain, of rain moving through the gutters. She quivered, which was the change in her blood, and then water was coming out onto the towel, quickly followed by a heavier substance that saw it darken.

I closed up her womb and flattened down her stomach. It took me some moments to button her dress. I looked at her wedding band and tweaked it out of its groove. It had stained the root of her finger a mossy green.

I took away the sopping towel and pushed it under the couch. It would stain the carpet. It had dripped on my dress. I hadn't thought to bring in a bowl.

With her underwear back around her hips and her dress straightened, I roused her.

—Well. You should feel better—cooler—right away, and you'll notice the other changes in a day or less. Once your body catches onto the change in your blood.

I put my hands over the stains in my lap.

—Oh, Ada.

She was laughing as she sat up, keeping her knees together and pointing her bunched toes toward her shoes. Laughing like she hadn't a care. The fine wrinkles around her eyes deepened in time to her irises flaring.

Her eyes were a dark, deep green. The color reminded me of the patch of ground 'round the side of the house. That sliver of earth the sun never hits, where the barest hint of moss festers in the wet shade.

Agatha Bond

I liked them fine. They could always do something for you. You always left feeling better.

It was the burying I couldn't get my head around.

In the ground. Not dead, just asleep—and for days.

I used to worry that something would go wrong and I'd *wake up* buried. Wake up *dead*.

That was the only thing.

Well. That and talking to them afterward. About what they'd seen.

How do you talk to someone who's been inside you?

Who's seen more of you than you've seen of yourself?

Father met Lorraine in the hall and I lifted the sagging towel into my lap and carried it up to the bathroom, making a sac out of the front of my dress. It landed without ceremony in the bath and pooled toward the drain. I pulled my soiled dress over my head and tossed it in too, and quickly all the cloth stewed into one. I heard her on the porch, heard a car in the drive.

Father came and stood in the doorway.

—Well?

—The usual. It was fine.

—What did you tell her?

—The usual. It was all the usual.

—She's coming back next week.

I leaned forward to turn on the tap. It sputtered at first, the smell of the old drains filling up the small damp room.

—Why?

—She wants to keep going with it. To keep getting flushed out.

—But it's all gone.

—She's set on it. Says she'll pay the same each time.

The water was coming strong now and I rolled my eyes.

—Father.

—She kept saying how she never felt better.

—You wouldn't let this pass if it was you who had to sit with her.

—There are worse ways to spend time.

*   *   *

And so Lorraine kept coming back for what she called her "treatment."

It was dull work, in that it was no work at all. I put her to sleep and waited a little while, sometimes singing a tune that would see her wake up cool.

As I've said, women Cures wanting their change sped up wasn't uncommon—the same women who went back to work when their newborns were still gasping for air. But Lorraine had never worked in the fields. Mr. Languid had had his own land. She'd no reason to put a rush on anything.

Her work had been what the other women called "clipped-wing work," which also meant there were habits she couldn't shake. She was determined, for instance, to soothe us and feed us. To give us things we didn't need.

It was a quiet time of year, with autumn's onset seeing less work in the fields and Cures more eager to spend time among themselves, so often once she woke up she could see no reason to leave.

—No other visitors today, Ada?

And then she'd lie back on the couch and shuffle through the box of postcards she carried around, telling me she brought them especially for me. With her knees gathered up to her chest I'd watch her finger their soft edges, and one day it struck me that Lorraine was the first Cure I'd ever known who'd once lived elsewhere. Her eyes had not always fallen first thing on our lemony horizon, and she'd not spent all her summers taking heed of the terra-cotta ground.

The postcards were inscribed with quick notes in colored ink, from Lorraine to Lorraine, mentioning to her future self the pastries of a particular street and the cobblestones of another, a corner where hems were lifted and soles peeled from their shoes. She was always turning to me and starting stories she couldn't finish, flapping a hand whenever a name escaped her, the unlit cigarette between her fingers losing its tobacco in fluttering slivers of yellow and brown.

Or else she'd busy herself around the house. Her body wakeful and well, loud and unyielding. I can hear them still, the *sounds* she made: the harsh spittle sound rocking across her tongue and clinging to her teeth, the pimpled skin of her inner thighs shifting against one another like the sheaths of a winter dress, her breasts damply filling the cups of her brassiere, like wet leaves tightly packed in a drain. The sigh of her body sinking into the cushions while her hair, falling away from her face, gave up its lacquered curls.

I found myself nodding along to the constant hum of her thoughts and catching sight of her bright, bright dreams.

She never wanted to go.

Often I figmented other imminent Cures to shift her.

Perhaps more than the noises she made and the hot white sun, those weeks are marked for me still by a taste of blood— *everywhere*, a taste of blood. Like the air was filled with copper flakes.

Her flesh is somewhere torn. Her blood is landing in my mouth.

I kept a hand at my throat, fearful of swallowing the wilted violet tang.

And I was tired. All the time.

Too tired, even, to dream.

Each night I'd lie down and begin to think of Samson, convince myself I caught his scent, and then there'd come a creak across Lorraine's shoulders.

Her gut-gurgle bubbling.

Her squeak-lung wheeze.

I'd push it to one side and think of Samson's hands, the bulge of his shoulders. I'd put my hands over my ears as though the sounds weren't seeded inside my own head and imagine him coming back up from The Ground.

I was tracking a piece of cotton, matted and thick, up the length of the lawn. It was headed toward the trees and it struggled over the long and scratching grass.

I walked a little way behind it, the shift I wore rising up over my knees.

Follow me, follow me.

It made a whistling sound, the cotton. The way a man whistles, hard and through straight teeth. I crouched and watched it bob a moment longer from stalk to stalk, to the occasional thistle stem, and then I heard a voice.

It was Fred Languid lamenting over a stillborn calf, and I was no longer in our garden but in the Languids' sodden barn and I looked down at myself and saw I was Lorraine.

The dream was a dream of Lorraine's, rooted in a spring-time some fifteen years before.

Opening my eyes I saw the sun was almost up and tasted the blood-taste strong in my mouth.

I went to the bathroom and spat, spat, spat.

—You and your father seem so rarely to speak.

—Often there isn't much to say.

—It's a funny way you have, of living together.

I don't know what she got from this back-and-forth between us. She was eager, I suppose, for some sign we were even a little bit alike. When she grew tired of asking after Father she'd say

—Tell me about your day.

Never mind whether or not she'd seen me throughout it, and I'd tell her what I could. Of the changes I'd seen in plants, of the growing weight to the air. She'd look at me with pity creasing the skin around her eyes.

—Season's changing, I suppose.

Thinking *Dull girl, dull girl. What a nonsense life you're living.*

All old women, I know, were at one time young.

These afternoons spent sitting next to her while she slept, I started wondering how she'd die and where she'd be put to

133

ground—not The Ground of our cramped garden, but those stretches kept sacred by Cures. Those stretches Father said we must never enter. Throughout my childhood he told me

—We leave the graveyards be.

—But why?

—Because they'll think we're there to make them well, and then they'll sit up.

—Sit up? In their graves?

—All their heads will come up over the soil, all asking to be the first saved.

One day the heat was such that she lay down on the couch right away. One hand over her face, the other fanning her breasts. The car hadn't even left the drive and already she was saying

—Oh, put me out, Ada! Put me out! This heat! I don't know how you stand it.

So I put my hand over her eyes and she was gone right away. Her mouth slack, her chin doubling into her neck. She hadn't even taken her shoes off; only one heel was unsheathed from her worn leather shoe and her stockings were wetly gathered 'round her knees. I couldn't keep looking at her. It was too much. The look and the smell of her. I went out on the porch and sat on the steps, thinking thoughts of Samson with my knees knocking and my head in my hands.

Long time in the desert.

Long time long time.

I looked at my feet, my toes weathered with dust, counted ten breaths, and got up to go inside again.

Back in the house the air smelled sweeter and I thought

I'll wake her and be stern with her, tell her we've another Cure.

I tripped a little over something on the floor: Lorraine's shoes, Lorraine's stockings.

Lorraine herself was gone.

The couch, where she'd been, ruffled and sagging.

My insides turned liquidy and quick. Where was she? And how had she woken on her own?

If Father sees, if Father sees . . .

I went into the kitchen, into the pantry, the toilet, back into the kitchen, and then: from the corner of my eye, a white spot moving. She was walking over the lawn. Right over the lawn. Bobbing slowly up and down like the cotton I'd seen in her dream.

I'd never seen a Cure gone past The Burial Patch. It looked like the sun and moon side by side in the sky.

Her feet, outside of their stockings, had a yellow tinge. I opened my mouth to call to her but again thought of Father, still unknowing, and then she was gathering up her dress— bunching it at the hem. She carried on, away from the house, deeply curving the arches of her feet like a dancer might, or like a woman about to step into a too-tight shoe.

When she stopped she bent her knees, letting them splay to either side.

The Ground will take her.

I went out the back door but she had already lowered to The Ground, hoisted her dress up further.

She was all contentment, all swagger.

She turned from me to show the house her buttocks, all pale and quiver, naked of their usual skein of aged silk and frayed lace.

She squatted, deeply. Paused.

The urine left her in an even streak. The sound of it on the grass, the crackling dry lawn.

Father will hear it.

It felt loud as a storm.

She stood up straight again, turned slow—too slow—and walked back toward me.

—Lorraine?

Coming back toward the house her face was blank, the skin 'round her jaws drooping. Lifting her knees high, one calf in front of the other, each the color of clotted cream.

—Lorraine? Are you awake, Lorraine?

She brushed by me and I could only follow her easy gait into the sitting room, where she lay back down on the couch and settled herself. Closed her eyes and started her deep-sleep-breath.

I could see her nipples toughening through the cloth of her dress.

When I woke her she'd looked at me and was herself.

When she left the house she was entirely herself.

I went to bed early so as not to speak with Father, who I was sure would hear the nervous rattle inside me. I only dared go outside the next day, once morning came with its spare and pale blue sky.

I went and stood on the grass. Looked down at where Lorraine had been squatting.

It was still so early the wooden parts of the house had yet to start groaning, resisting the heat after the cool of the night.

I could smell it. The yellow tang.

What had happened to her while she slept? What had taken seed? And what if Father noticed this patch of yellow in the middle of the lawn?

I pulled at the hem of my dress, felt on my shoulders the keen eyes of a magpie, strutting behind me on the roof.

Later that day, we were brought a young boy Cure.

Cormac Kent was the mildest kind of ill: when he ate, he felt a little fire inside.

Just as well, I thought, knowing I was too tired and fretful for anything more testing.

He was small, freckled, and pale but he spoke pushing down on his throat, willing his voice to deepen. He was at that age of acting out the motions he'd learned in the company of men. Hence his insistence on shaking Father's hand, and his hard squint at my chest.

—You go with Miss Ada, Cormac, his mother said. A small woman who wore a hat.

I took him to the porch and told him to rock in the chair we kept there until he began to feel cool. He kept his eyes on me while he leaned into his feet and set the chair to creaking, the old boards beneath whining hard and yellow and long.

It was rare for us to take a Cure outside, but often the younger ones were too tightly wound upon arrival. I rested against the house and counted the creaks, thinking after thirty-five or so he might be ready to open, but I lost count— kept thinking about Lorraine and the yellowed grass.

—I've been hearing all about you—

—What's that?

But when he spoke he'd a child's phrasing again.

—We hear all sortsa things 'bout you.

I had my hands deep in my pockets.

—I'd say you do.

I'd keep my gaze on the driveway as long as the boards carried on creaking. I wondered if this was in fact a hotter summer, and if it was the weather that saw Cures getting evermore strange.

—I hear your girl parts are on the wrong way 'round.

—Yessir, and upside down. You feeling any cooler yet?

The creaking stopped.

—I'm just here because my mamma says you can fix me, but I'd never let you inside of me. No way. You kill us kids so you can eat us. You eat up our arms and then you leave our legs for Sister Eel.

—If you don't want to be cured then you go tell your mother so because it doesn't matter to me whether you can keep your dinner down.

It took me a moment to realize he wasn't moving, that he was staying perfectly still. I'd put him to sleep without touching him—without meaning to at all.

His mouth was a little way open, his eyes out of focus. He looked like he'd drowned and was floating in the water that killed him.

I could smell the hormones splicing inside him. I could smell the sweat in his glands that had yet to disperse and stain his brown pressed pants and yellow shirt, stretched thin about the shoulders by his brothers who'd worn it before him.

Poised and helpless. Captive bird.

I unbuttoned his shirt and quickly, without my usual care, opened up his stomach and squatted low to look inside. There were indeed some sparks flaring along his gut, which had in fact worn dangerously fine; I plucked them like berries, one by one, and threw them like darts into the porch. They left little scorched marks on the wood. The tune was a strained one. It wanted to catch on a loop, to jolt and skip, even as I welded his skin back together in a thin line.

—Cormac, wake up.

He didn't move, and his pupils were the smallest of pricks in the center of a muddy haze.

I bent down to look him in the face and said again

—*Wake up.*

And this time he did. Looking pained and afraid.

—You had some fire in you, but it's passed.

I leaned in the door and called to Father and then rested my back against the house again. Cormac Kent didn't speak, only sat in the chair with his shirt undone. He looked down at himself and then his child's hands began fumbling with the buttons of his shirt, which was very worn and much too large. He did them up unevenly, his collar sagging, and I knew then—by his harsh breath and flickering eyes—that he'd not slept while I was inside him. He'd been stilled only, and very much awake.

When Father came to the door Mrs. Kent was busy in her purse behind him. They carried on speaking and so missed the look, already waning, on her son's face. Father was looking at me and I was telling him with a nod that the illness was gone.

I don't know how we were paid because I kept watching the boy, thinking he'd surely evidence some sign. But he only looked at the ground, at the pockmarked wood, his baby mouth a little way open. One over the other he laid his freckled hands across his stomach, which I knew now to be a whitewashed pale. I knew also that he'd wait until he was home and alone to cry. And that of my witch's hands rummaging around his gut he'd never say a word.

Never let you inside of me, no way.

Father's idle words. Mrs. Kent already inside the car. Already simpering at her son.

A few days later I was lying in the grass while the morning was still mild. Thinking of Samson beneath me and pressing my hips into The Ground, rolling my shoulders and turning my head side to side. I could feel him there, and it soothed me.

Father came out of the house behind me. I heard his steps: soft and slow. He stood beside me and I felt his shadow across my knees.

—Lorraine is here.

—Already?

I rolled away from him, onto my side. I'd decided Lorraine's waking up was a sign she'd been put to sleep too many times, that she was growing a kind of callous toward it. But I couldn't tell Father. Couldn't tell him I'd left a Cure unattended. And I didn't know what I'd do with her today, if I couldn't make her sleep.

Behind my eyes I saw Samson's thighs, their muscle-bulge.

—She's been acting strangely.

I clenched a little. I knew he hadn't seen her in the garden and that he thought a tomcat had yellowed the grass. He'd

140

poured a certain broth over the poisoned patch to help it
regain its green.

I snorted, made myself sound disinterested—calm—and
said

—She's a Cure.

—She's been saying things that don't make sense. Like
she's had a fit and her brain's misfiring.

—She's just talking about her old life. It doesn't make
sense because she always starts in the middle.

—It's not stories, just sentences.

—Like what?

—"Long time in the desert," "Not a bad man."

I opened my eyes and looked up to Father's face but he
wasn't looking at me. He was looking at The Ground. I kept
very still.

—Must be going senile.

—Bit before her time.

—. . . Should I look inside her head today?

He rubbed at his scalp. The grey-blond hair flickering.
Kept staring and staring at The Ground.

—No . . . no, maybe it is just her memory looping.

Still, his eyes on The Ground, crinkled—almost closed.
Then, eventually,

—Be careful out here, Ada. Even in sunshine. Everything's feeling strange.

Lorraine was smoking and looking out the window, one knee
rested on the couch.

—How are you feeling today, Lorraine?

She turned around quick, smiling.

—Morning, Ada. Feeling fine, just fine.

—You want to lie down?

Which she did, stubbing the cigarette out gently so she could return to it again.

When I put her to sleep she twitched a little, which wasn't unusual. Her lips made themselves thick and her eyelids shriveled shut. I sat back on my knees and watched her. Waited.

It didn't take long.

Her mouth came a little way open, and there was a rattling sound.

It sounded like her spine was shaking and the sound was coming up through her. I'd never heard such a sound, a body trying to ground some portion of itself to dust.

—Why are you trembling, Lorraine?

And then her head snapped back and her mouth opened fully. I could see the large teeth near the root of her tongue gleaming wet and silver where the air had not yet seen the spittle dried. She opened her eyes and they were wide, unseeing. She reached up to me, her square fingers carrying the lightest touch of yellow.

—Come down to me, Ada.

Her mouth moved with a roundness that didn't match her words.

—Why will you not come down?

—Come down where, Lorraine? You're right here.

For a terrible moment I thought she meant for me to kiss her or embrace her in some way. I felt a simmering warmth in my loins that sickened me.

—What's happening to you, Lorraine?

—You keep me waiting on you like a dog, Ada.

That swirling warmth in my groin. Sweet and thick. *No*, I thought. *No.*

My loins filling up with sweet wet hurt and that pincer heat inside me.

And then Lorraine spoke again but her voice was not quite her own.

—It's been a long time in the desert.

I went outside. I was shaking, I think.

I felt a stream inside me was quickening.

I meant to taste the hot dry air and wash out my mouth.

I've dreamt it, I've dreamt it. I've dreamt him too strong and called up some strangeness. Made the words take root like a growth inside her.

I stopped on the bottom of the stairs and hit at my groin. Made a fist and wedged my hand into the softness there, around the carmine muscle and bone.

My eyes and throat were hurting, but no wet came.

Maybe I'm crying.

Could be I was crying in that dry, soundless way I'd seen take over certain Cures—their mouths wide open but with little sound, their eyes shining but only giving up the thinnest tears.

In bed that night I kept the lamp on beside me.

Chill after chill ran through me. If I closed my eyes I saw Lorraine standing over me, stealing Samson's words and gleaning something of his tongue.

Had I channeled some of my want into her aged, damp body?

Was my need of him so warm and alive it took up space in the nearest Cure?

A pain behind my eyes. The soreness of needful sleep. And the ache in me still pounding, still raw from having been so stirred. The bruised longing there telling me what I knew but couldn't fathom: that what was happening to Lorraine was not my doing at all.

Quick haze of a dream.

Of lying down on the lawn.

Of a magpie circling.

Lorraine was due and I met her on the porch. Father was working in the garden, down at the far end near the trees. She'd driven herself, for a change.

—How you feeling today, Lorraine?

—Oh, I'm wonderful.

Reaching for her handbag in the back seat.

—Slept like a dream.

—I see.

Inside the house she made for the sitting room, but I said

—Some tea, before we start?

—Oh, how nice! Yes!

She sat at the kitchen table and crossed her fleshy legs. Put her hands on the table and started to play with a bracelet, undoing the clasp.

—So, you slept well?

Kettle on the stove.

—Yes! Well. Just the occasional strange dream.

—What did you dream of?

Taking the tea leaves from their tin.

Though she was tired she kept her shoulders back; her breasts seemed to me a touch higher, a touch more pointed and firm. Whatever was happening to her, it agreed with her.

—It really was strange . . . I was deep in a swamp or something like it. But I couldn't swim, and I didn't drown . . .

Damn. Damn, damn, damn.

—Well, why don't we just sit here a moment.

Looking out at the garden, the lawn looking so harmless and smooth. Father with his back to us. Squatting, standing again.

—I'm not keeping you today?

—No, Lorraine, you're my only Cure.

I brought the tea to the table. A teapot I had to wipe clean of dust and two porcelain cups. I poured her a cup and looked at her face, her sagging jaw, her pockmarked brow. She was twitching. The muscles in her throat shot up and down like little bolts of lightning and her lips pulled back from her teeth. I said

—I'm afraid we don't have milk . . . or sugar.

She leaned forward and lashed the full cup toward me so it landed scalding in my lap. I felt it sizzle and burn while I looked at her, looked out the window. Father was still looking away, but Lorraine was leaned over the table now, her hands fisted up and knuckle-down on the wood. Wheezing, her shoulders forward. And then she slumped back, nearly knocking the chair.

—Oh, Ada, little Ada—I am sorry, I don't know what—

—That's all right, Mrs. Languid, why don't we go into the sitting room.

And she lay back on the couch and kept on rasping until I put my hand over her eyes.

I didn't open her, just let her sleep, putting my hand over her face and singing the song harder to make sure the slumber stayed deep. After a little while I lifted up my dress to remove the burnt skin where it was coming away in thin, papery layers. Shimmering where it caught the light. Lorraine kept sleeping, but even in her sleep I saw her muscles stutter and leap.

Not my desire. Not any of my feelings at all.

Damn, damn, damn.

Gilda Flynn

I haven't thought about Samson Wyde in years. Him and his sister, we used to call them "rumor-rich." He disappeared and then she was gone a month or two after.

No doubt they're off living in sin somewhere, thinking us all fools.

From my bedroom I heard a car approaching. I assumed it was Lorraine, thinking she could call on us at her leisure. I was still thinking what to do with her, how to temper Samson in The Ground.

But it was Olivia.

I looked out my window and saw her in the drive, went quickly downstairs and met her on the porch, stopped her on the steps.

She was shining across her collar and her eyes were twitching at their corners, where the soft lid ran into the sides of her face. Pretty, pretty woman.

—Hi, Mrs. Claudette. I'm afraid I can't see you now. It really is better you make an appointment—

—You seen my brother?

Taking deep breaths through her nose like she'd been tracking his scent and it had led her here.

—No, I haven't.

Looking over my shoulder.

—Your father here?

—Yes.

—Has he seen him?

—He hasn't been here, Mrs. Claudette. Would be unusual if he had.

—He's gone. He's gone and with no word left behind him.

—Has he been gone a long time?

—I'd like to ask your father if he's seen him.

—Father gets angry when people waste his time.

She looked back to the truck, thinking, and I kept my face very still and hoped hard that Father wouldn't hear anything she said, anything that would entice him to come outside. I said

—I don't know why you think he'd be here, Mrs. Claudette. Your brother is nothing but healthy.

She kept on looking at the truck; her lips came apart and let loose some unhappy laughter. I was pushing her now, making her angry enough to show it. I couldn't help myself. I liked seeing her upset, liked knowing things she didn't know. A warm shiver ran through me.

—Besides, I thought you were afraid of him.

Those soft lids, the blood inside them quickening.

—Mrs. Claudette? I thought you were afraid of your brother?

She settled back into herself, into her heels. The whole of her lengthening. Still looking away from me. I could see her neck, tautening.

—You just let me know if you see him.

I was leaning forward on the porch. I made sure my shoulders looked soft, made sure my voice matched hers.

—I surely will.

Another deep breath and then she was turning on the step, but only halfway. Looking down at her belly, she said

—It never felt wrong to me, you know.

The wood under my elbows was itchy, suddenly. Itchy and hard.

—I'd have stopped, if it felt wrong.

—I don't know what you mean.

Slow smile. Still looking down at herself. The spit on her teeth shining.

—I would have. I'd have stopped.

Her smile like a slice in her face. As always, so pleased with herself. Nothing could stop her from feeling pleased with herself.

—Sometimes our feelings aren't the best indication of what we should be doing.

I knew right away I'd made a mistake in speaking.

She laughed, loud and fully, looked up at me, smiling before turning to go.

—So long, Miss Ada.

The look on her face resounding clear as her laughter that carried on smarting my ears in the hot buzzing day.

Pot, kettle. Look who's talking. Hypocrite.

Liar.

She knew enough to suspect he'd told me what she'd done.

Enough to suspect he might be here.

But she didn't know everything. Not by half. Nothing was wrong. Nothing had come undone.

Father came outside and started sniffing at the air.

—Who was here?

—Mrs. Claudette.

—Woman is highly strung. You said she was an easy Cure.

—She was. Must be the baby doing things to her. Sending all the wrong sparks to her brain.

Wiping his hands, moving up to his elbows.

—She didn't mention her brother?

—No.

Her smile as she looked down at herself, looked down at her belly. The way she looked at the high hard mound.

—No, I said again. They don't get along.

Maria Claudette

My son was a good man but he was an innocent.

We begged him not to marry that girl.

If ever there was a girl with a snake inside . . .

Like I say, we begged him.

And then he got sick, and he died.

We couldn't take his name away from her but we could take the house.

One thing I *could not abide* was her staying on in that house.

Chuckling and slithering around.

The next day: more unexpected visitors.

Another young boy Cure.

Just as the sky started to color with evening and the patio stones were turning cool.

I was in bed, trying to stop thinking about Olivia, trying to think of a way to keep Lorraine out of the house. To stop her from *wanting* to come to the house. Wondering when it was Cure women started taking up so much of my time.

So when I heard the car, I didn't move. When I heard Father's heavy steps in the hall, I didn't move.

When he called to me, it struck me that his voice was full of rattle.

They were coming through the front door before I reached the bottom of the stairs; two men, one of them carrying a soft, yielding body. Behind them came a younger man holding a woman by her elbows. They were all of them dressed in grey and black, and this last man was wet and hiding his shivers.

I didn't know the boy's name. I wouldn't know until later, when it seemed likely not only his name but his face would come to haunt me later.

Oliver James.

They rested him against the cushions of that same lagging couch that had seen so many bodies gone to sleep. The woman had knelt and began to rearrange the boy's hair so that it more evenly framed his face. She was looking at Father, who was kneeling beside her, and with eyes on his face she touched her son's small jacket, the lapels made heavy with water.

Without preamble the men gathered themselves in an orderly line on the couch's far side. I thought *They might be at church*, and then scolded myself for thinking in mocking terms.

Mrs. James had set to rocking now, gently bumping her forehead onto and off of her son's sodden chest. Her hands were knotted and pressed into the midriff of her dress. From under her clothes I heard the creasing of soft, maternal flesh.

He was not her only child, but he was the youngest.

One of the older men was speaking: the boy had left the field where he was helping his uncles and brothers, and he had fallen into Sister Eel Lake. It was the wet man who had heard the splash of interrupted water. Of course, we knew without their saying what had happened; there was such a stench of the lake, and beneath their talk I could hear the wet smack of drowning.

—Ada, come look at the boy.

It was the first time I'd worked with the family present. I knelt between the weeping Mrs. James and Father with all of the men looking down at my hands, all of them milky-skinned. *They must be from the valley*, which was on the far side of the fields and held some thirty people. They had a close way of living together, and the positioning of the hills put most of their days in the shade. Hence the churned look to their skin, rather than the scrubbed complexions of those who lived in town.

I started right away as there was no need to put him to sleep.

Pulling up his faded shirt, I made an arrow of my hand and went inside him, which made Mrs. James cry harder. I worked both of my hands beneath the skin and under his rib cage, and she cried harder still.

The swallowed water started to gather in my hands and I sang to send it away. Mrs. James and the men, her other sons, took turns looking up as the ceiling darkened and dripped with heavy, gluttonous lake water drops.

My thoughts did something they shouldn't have done, which was wander. I couldn't stop picturing the boy's brother diving and surfacing, thrashing in the water until the lake was riddled with foam. I saw a stark image of Sister Eel wrapped some seven times around the small body, her snout near his face.

I moved my hands and worked the water out of him, and once it was gone there was only stillness inside of him.

He had died in the lake, and now he was here on our couch with his eyelashes clung together in bands of three or four.

Still I kept my hands moving, hoping to feel in the fibrous lining a glimmer of breath I might fan into gasping and see him sputter, jolt inside his sodden clothes.

I kept on, pushing water out of his lungs and into the ceiling, my hair and shoulders slick from the dripping water and Oliver James, his face held by his mother, made doubly wet again by its fall. I kept on until the quiet in the room was like a hand around my throat, and I realized my wrists were sore, which had never happened before.

—He's gone too far.

I spoke loudly to cover the wet, sliding sound of my hands coming back to the air.

Mrs. James said nothing but rolled up her shoulders, slowly.

I kept seeing things I didn't want to see.

The ringlets of hair on the sides of his face were so slick and fine they might've been painted.

Since he'd been laid out on the couch his eyes had turned a deeper shade of green.

He'd a freckle near his mouth that would have been folded into his cheek whenever he smiled.

A hum of confused muttering from the men as they remembered Tabatha Sharpe: a frail baby brought back from the bloody pool of her mother's panicked womb—surely, *surely*, I could fashion a means of revival for this small child? If I could pluck Tabatha out of thin air, and this boy was here in front of me, with everything about him intact . . . ?

And Father only looked at me in a way that sent his thoughts clear into my head.

This is the cost of your running around, Ada.

Oliver James. Quiet little boy, bathed deep in the green of the lake. Already a body, instead of a boy. No more than a streak of light skin and dark hair between us. His cheeks still puffed as though with stubborn, petulant breath rather than the sickly bloat of Sister Eel Lake, beaten from above by the rain. Cheeks his mother kept on stroking, thinking she might alleviate their swell and bring back her small, drowned son.

Had I the will to touch him again I might have strummed a quick tune of feathers, with which to close his eyes.

* * *

—You could have saved that boy.

I sat down on the couch, still wet.

This room will forever stink of the lake.

That night, of course, I didn't sleep.

Father was irked with me; it had been a long time since we'd lost a Cure and he felt this one had been lost needlessly. I told him over and over that the boy was too far gone, was already dead, but as the sheets turned knotted and damp around me I wondered if indeed my strength was dripping away.

If Samson trying to work his way into Lorraine was taking a toll on me I couldn't yet fathom.

My eyes grew heavy and I dreamt half-awake dreams of Oliver James climbing out of the lake or riding Sister Eel like a mare.

And then I dreamt, briefly, of Olivia, who by this time must've given birth.

I was in the kitchen with the back door and all the windows open so the smell of rain came in strong. Wet soil and spattered leaves. The heat from the stove was warming my belly and I fanned myself with my dress. I was still tired from Oliver James and my every movement seemed slow. I'd been stirring the pot so long I knew, even after I stopped, the motion would keep on in my shoulder.

I heard Lorraine's car in the drive. Early, as was her habit now. I thought, *Must be the fact of her coming so often. He's used to her—he can sniff her out*, looking at the boiling pot and wanting to dip my hands inside. *You need a plan.*

But what to do? Even if I'd wanted to, I couldn't bring up Samson. Only Father could force anything in that part of The Ground—my putting him there had worked only because it chimed with the weather.

And I didn't want him to come up before he was ready.

No matter how long it took.

Lorraine was coming up the steps and, before I could put the spoon down, letting herself inside. She was the only Cure to ever do so, and despite myself it made me sad that she thought of us as her family. She'd come here looking for something we couldn't give her, some kind of closeness she could draw on while she lay in bed. Lay in the dark, alone.

All she'd gotten was Samson slipping inside her to catch a glimpse aboveground.

I called

—Be right with you, Lorraine.

—Ada.

I knew right away: Her voice that wasn't her voice. Her voice with a hot tremor inside it. I turned around and there he was, a too-big hand in an ill-fitting glove. The shoulders rolling forward, the slight tilt to the hips.

—What have you done to me?

The dress she'd put on that morning was sodden, damply creased about the hips and breasts. Her hair was falling 'round her face, reddy-grey frame all tendril and wisp. Again,

—What have you done to me?

—I'm making us time. More time.

He laughed and it was not Lorraine's laugh but not his

160

either. Only a quick dislodging in the throat. A few steps toward me, uncertain and slow.

—You bring me up.

—You'll come up as soon as you're ready. The Ground'll know.

—Now.

I leaned back on the counter. It was such a sad sight, his beautiful body kicking and squirming inside her. And Lorraine; disfigured, and perhaps the most alive she'd ever been.

—Now, Ada.

Close to me now and putting Lorraine's hands on my waist, and the touch too familiar. The heat of the stove slicking up my back. Her lips so close I could see clearly their fine lines and whiskery corners. Cigarette breath landing on my mouth. I said

—The Ground will keep you safe. It'll cure you of the hurt Olivia put in you.

It was like he'd been poured inside her, hot and molten, and she was squirming so as not to get burned. Every time she moved he showed through a little, pushing at the seams.

A wild dog snapping.

—I can't stay down there.

—It's not forever.

Lorraine's face wrinkling around her mouth and nose, dense center of a rose.

—Bring me up, Ada.

—I can't.

—Your father—

—The Ground will know. The Ground will be able to tell. Was Lorraine in there still? While he spoke through her?

The first sign I should have taken heed of: her knee giving out from under her. Jerking, spasming. He carried on talking. Couldn't feel what he was doing to her.

—What have you done? Why—

—I'm fixing what Olivia did to you. Isn't that what you wanted? Isn't that why you kept on asking me to look inside?

The second sign: the moisture coming through her dress.

Her body doing something it hadn't done for years and, lacking milk, producing some other liquid long since spoiled inside her.

—Dammit, Ada! This is not what I wanted! No!

Trying to make a fist but his will not quite making it down into Lorraine's soft, slow fingers.

By now Father was standing in the hall, looking into the kitchen, looking at me over Lorraine's frizzing hair. He'd been upstairs but Samson was shouting, his voice coming thick over Lorraine's tongue,

—I thought we were leaving. Leaving together. I thought *that* was our plan.

I was found out, my scheming undone in the kitchen with its blackened pots and unwashed floor. Undone and suddenly unremarkable, with the breadth of Father's shoulders in the doorway stealing the light from the room. Probably Samson mistook Father for clouds crowding the sun, because he kept talking to me—mewling, every few words his voice turned to squeak.

—What have you done, Ada? What have you done?

The stains on the front of her dress, pooling now. Sticking to her.

I hope she's not awake.

Her jaw moving as though her tongue had swollen in her mouth and Samson's words coming out of her with a strange, dull echo. A light bubbling on her lips making me think of the foam the river made when no rain had come to flush its innards clean. The flaccid flesh of her throat trembling, unable to keep up with her breath and, finally, her temples giving off a hard, buzzing sound. A bee trapped under a mug.

I don't know if a younger woman would have managed better or if there's any way to survive such a thing.

In any case, something somewhere burst, and she fell.

When she fell she fell hard and her left knee, the knee she came down on, cracked.

The sound that came out of her mouth could have been either of them.

Not quite low, not quite high.

A sweep of loam on the tiles: the track he'd made in leaving her.

And then it was Father talking.

A new voice, but the same questions.

—*What have you done, Ada?*

—*Ada, what have you done?*

It seemed a long time passed, and still we stood looking at Lorraine on the floor.

—Dammit, Ada.

—I know.

—He's not a fox. He's not a bird.

—I know.

—How long has he been down there?

—. . . Two weeks.

—No more?

—No.

—Why have you done this?

On the floor in front of me her body was leaking its last few dregs. Her mouth, her ears, and her eyes. The slow, shiny spread come out beneath her skirt. And then: she kicked a little. The hem of her dress showed us more of her pale, damp thigh. I said

—Because it wasn't enough.

If he'd been a Cure he might have sighed, rubbed at his eyes. But he only looked at me.

—Enough?

—The days going on and on. Dipping in and out of Cures. I need to keep him and if I'm going to keep him I need to fix him. Need to keep him safe from his sister for a time.

Father's brow churning. I was giving too much away.

—You were right. He's sick. But it's her that put it there.

Looking at me hard, not willing to be distracted.

—How'd you do it? Get him down there?

—It was just the rain. When the storm came. I just . . .

And I made a motion with my hand.

—But this—?

Staring at Lorraine's hurt body. Her mouth slack and an oily film escaping her eyes.

—That he's done alone.

Her spittle tapping onto the floor.

—We can't fix her?

—No. There's too much here I haven't seen.

His hands on his hips. His body so large.

—Besides. If she remembered any of this, ever said anything about any of this . . . they'd burn us down.

An ache shooting in quick red lines up my spine.

—So we carry her upstairs, let her die in her own time?

He snorted.

—Little late to be treating Lorraine kindly.

He was walking around her, looking at her from every side.

—All we can do is put her to ground and let her go quietly.

—After we put her to sleep?

—She *is* sleeping, Ada, look at her.

Lorraine's eyes thick with water, neither open nor closed.

—Can't we leave her in one of the rooms?

—No. The Ground.

Looking down, speaking into his chest,

—He'll have been worked upon, you know. Down there.

I looked at him with my eyes, careful not to move my face.

—That's the point.

Looking over my head and into the garden.

—You don't know what you've done, Ada.

—I'm not all to blame.

—You ready to say something about him? A man so good
and wholesome you had to sink him in The Ground?

—Not him.

My hands, where he couldn't see them, inside my pockets,
pinching my thighs. I said

—You must've known I'd get lonely.

He looked at me and his whole face went soft, so soft he
might have started laughing.

—Not likely what comes back up will give a damn if
you're lonely, Ada.

Lifting Lorraine up easily, muttering to himself

—Lonely. Lonely. Need to have a heart, to be lonely.

That night we buried Lorraine. Father came out of the house and the patio door whinnied shut behind him. His shoulders shone heavily, their smooth skin catching the white glare of the moon.

Lorraine: humming in her sleep.

I moved my toes against the side of her head, which was silhouetted and obscured with the swinging light at the patio door. Father came closer and Lorraine began to move against my foot in the way a stray cat might scratch its back against the rough bark of a tree.

—Leave her be, Ada.

Sinking the shovel into The Ground. It smacked like a thirsty mouth, though we'd had much rain. I was surprised it didn't give off steam.

I looked at her hard, sniffed at the air.

He started digging.

I squatted next to Lorraine and the mud licked up toward my knees. My dress dipped deeper into the wet dirt.

Clung to me.

Stocking.

Pouch.

Glove.

From Lorraine's open mouth came a sound like a lone dove's coo and then she tried to roll onto her side, making swivel the slack rings of fat around her belly.

I stood up and felt her face with my foot and pushed down on the flat expanse of cheek, where the hard bars of her jaw clenched under the skin.

Father said nothing but lifted her up and carried her to the hole he'd made, saying it would be a long time before we could make use of that piece of ground again. Lorraine sagged heavily, filling up the angles of his arms while the cloth of her dress crinkled at her elbows and knees.

Once she'd been covered and Father had patted smooth the soil, it kept on moving, catching on her roving hips.

Back in the kitchen even the mismatched buttons of my dress seemed scalded by the heat as I brought them through their cat-eye holes. I let the patterned cloth hang from my fist and watched its slow twirl, sodden and limp, dropping it in the milky-watered basin. It made a thirsty, gulping sound, diminishing for a moment the soapy swirls that had formed so thickly over Father's shirt and my smock from the day before. It would take hours for the chalk-colored pattern to settle again and work on this fresh batch of stains.

I took the towel from its hook on the back of the kitchen door and rubbed it over my legs, but in bed I still felt the crumbling of dried soil run over my feet when I kicked at the sheets.

My cheek on the pillow, I closed my eyes and said *I'm sorry, Lorraine, you had a few more years*, and that night and for two nights thereafter I heard her squirming around in the earth, her head rolling across her collar and the thin bones cracking in the tunnel of her neck.

Father, very pointedly, spent time only at the front of the house.

*   *   *

—You might say sorry, Ada, for the trouble you've caused.

—Do you remember when I took you out of The Ground? How happy I was to meet you?

When, at last, Lorraine abated, I heard her chest lower and stay there. The Ground had seen her expire, and now our days would fall back to their old rhythm and I could plan for my time with Samson. That faraway time.

I did wonder how we'd the three of us live in the same house, but then I'd years and years to think of a way. I hoped once Father met Samson again, risen up and altered, he'd forget his dislike and his distrust. See that he'd become like us and didn't have to be handled like a Cure.

It was unlikely, but still I hoped for it. And like I said, I'd years and years.

From the porch: watching Father heave Lorraine's car down the drive, the buffered skin of his back gleaming. Long, long strides, moving the little tin car into whatever ditch was closest and deepest.

And that was all we had to do.

Nobody ever came looking for her.

It was not a kind place for a woman to live alone.

*   *   *

A few days went by and we'd no Cures. Father was highly strung and couldn't sit still for long. The weather had turned dry so I'd sit out in the garden and sun my legs, lying on my belly and singing to Samson through The Ground. I was certain he could hear me and that he was forgiving me, that he was already feeling better for his time there. I thought

If this is how it's to be, the waiting, maybe I can manage. Maybe it's not so bad.

Clucking and stretching, rubbing my back in the grass. Telling him what everything looked like, the trees and the sun in the sky.

—Are you hot down there, Samson? Can you feel the midday heat?

A few times I caught Father looking at me from the kitchen window and knew he thought me obscene.

And then one morning Father came in from the garden and ran the kitchen tap. He was smeared up to his elbows in dirt.

—All right, we've a storm due.

Splashing his forearms and wetting his rolled sleeves. He said

—If it lasts as long as it's supposed to, I can manage.

I kept my eyes ahead, spied the angled limbs of a cricket on the lawn.

—You don't know how to do it.

—Of course I do.

—Father—

—He's coming up, Ada. He's a danger to us, down there. The Ground does what it pleases and nothing else besides.

—Isn't that a good thing? The longer we leave him, the more he'll be like us—

—There's no such thing as "like us."

—You said I couldn't keep him because he was sick. You said about Mr. Kault—

—If we'd have tried to cure Mr. Kault we'd have done all manner of things. You think you're fixing him. You're just leaving him to stew in what's wrong with him.

—I don't want him *fixed*, I only want him a little changed. Just enough so he's not tortured by the sick Olivia put inside him.

Because if he was all the way fixed he mightn't want me. Might take fright at me, choke at the thought of our being together.

Father was drying his hands now. His whole body waving me away, dismissing me.

—Next heavy rain he comes up.

A cold, slick tail flicking in my stomach. The sunshine bleaching everything. My whole world, faded.

—Can't we just wait and see?

He squinted at the cloth he was holding.

—You keep on refusing and I'll do it alone.

I was sitting at the table but felt like standing.

—Father—

—It's not just about what you want, Ada. A man like that could poison the earth for years.

A man like that.

A man.

—We'll bring him up and start fixing the mess you've made.

—How can it be a mess when it's exactly as I planned?

—Besides me finding out.

Biting into my cheek.

—Yes. Besides that.

—Storm tonight, and then we take him up tomorrow.

—No.

—Ada.

—You think you'll let him loose and he'll run for the hills and that'll be the end of it? You think he won't still want to be with me?

—. . . I think you overestimate your pull.

Cluck cluck cluck on my tongue.

—Besides, Ada, won't be up to him where he goes.

—What do you mean?

—What you think I mean.

—I don't know what you mean, 's why I'm asking you to say it.

—You've become a lot of things, but I know you've not become a fool.

—No. I won't do it.

Put him down like a dog too old, too blind. Take the life out of his fruit heart.

—You really think he'd ever look at you the same, Ada? What do you think is happening to him down there?

I put my hands flat on my lap. Pretended interest with the creases in my dress.

—It'll have been torture for him, Ada. You can't imagine. *Torture*.

We looked at each other and I thought about the changes I'd seen in him since I was a child: the thin, thin lines certain light showed up around his eyes. Otherwise he was the same.

When I was a child I'd sit on Father's shoulders and he'd walk me 'round the lawn, pointing out the plants I was made of. I played with the hair on top of his head and he put me in trees, up in the branches so that I couldn't get down. If I got frightened he'd say

—There's no use in fear, Ada.

And watch as I squirmed my way to the grass.

There's no use in lots of things, turns out.

Turns out once you find the thing you need, everything else falls away sharp and fast.

I put a hand on his chest, and he looked at me.

Looked *down* at me, our shared breath growing thick between us.

His big hands like bells at his sides.

It was a new kind of knowing in me, that I could hurt him. That my body was capable of damaging his. It was a new limb I'd grown for myself; to do him harm, to keep Samson safe.

There was a harsh creaking sound. A sound of bones made to stretch rather than right out breaking. He opened his mouth and I thought he might ask me to stop, but even if he had it was too late—once I started it felt like lying down to sleep, or like stepping into cool water. It felt like a curing but turned on its head, everything flowing hard in the wrong direction.

While it was happening one image came into my head and stayed there: a bird with one wing, flapping, convinced it could still take flight.

Behind my hand a wound had opened in his chest, and then spread. Even when I took my hand away it kept on spreading, making the sound a fire makes when the rain makes it spit but it carries on burning.

I looked inside him, inside his chest and the organs he kept there.

Saw his makeshift lungs.

His false heart.

I looked inside him and saw what he wanted for me: a half-life. A body barely stimulated, its urges only ever partially fulfilled. I looked at his face but he was looking over my head, into the garden, maybe thinking I'd drag him outside. Maybe thinking I'd bury him next to his father.

I'd assumed he was flesh and flesh throughout, held up with staffs of bone. But no, his insides were soft, and they came away in my hand, and the fluid that left him was not blood, of course, but a hearty crimson color, and certainly something that had been keeping him alive. The sound it made, coming out of his open chest and trickling to the floor, the soft patter of it on the tiles. A little cub suckling its mother's teat raw.

When I realized he was falling I thought *Don't fall toward me*.

And he didn't.

He fell to his side. His face on the tiles. Looking up at me from the same spot where Lorraine had lain and trembled.

Would I have done it sooner, if I'd known that I could? If I knew I could make him die, and if it had meant that Samson didn't need to go to ground?

Father had been surprised when he realized I needed to sleep. Been surprised that I dreamed.

Always asked me what I'd seen.

He'd presumed to know every part of me.

—When you were a child. The birds.

Olivia Wyde

You are the only precious thing.

    Whatever she says to you, what*ever* she or anyone else tries to make you believe, you laugh and look the other way.

    You know the truth now.

PART IV

Yes. The Ground is moving. Is ready to smack its tongue, to belch. The Ground is done with him, at last. Has moved through him and made him ready. Will he come up standing? Will he pull himself up with his honey-tan arms? I stand on the patio and try not to run to the part that's turning in on itself, a toothless mouth, the gums bearing down on the lips, massaging.

Such a long time to have waited and still I feel caught out. He will be the only thing to have changed. The house, the garden. The look and shape of my face.

All the same.

Such a long time.

But then: the time I've made.

Bethany Mills

I can't remember what time of year it was.

Just another hot month that felt like it was getting hotter.

I hadn't been able to make an appointment and I was getting desperate. Cruel, tight feeling in my low back and I knew from before, from another visit, that some important inside parts are kept there.

So I just went to the house, which I knew we were not supposed to do. Which I knew they very much *did not like*. But this hurt—I can't tell you, waking up in the night and a feeling like someone had taken a fistful of the skin there.

I got there in the morning, pulled myself up the steps, and knocked and knocked. At first I waited in between bouts of knocking, but then I just let my knuckles loose on the door because the pain was getting worse just standing there and the thought that they might not answer whipped something up in me. Not anger exactly but not miles away from anger either. When she came to the door I couldn't talk right away, had to wait till my breath was back.

—Miss Ada, I'm sorry for the racket—truly. But I couldn't make an appointment, and my back, Miss Ada, I know you said before I might have trouble when I was older, but—

I noticed her dress then. Small, creamy thing, but so green with stains she must have been rolling, and I mean *positively rolling*, in the grass. Dreaming hard and unkind dreams there on the lawn.

—Miss Ada, have you . . .

—Sorry I didn't hear you, Mrs. Mills, I was just napping in the garden.

I kept blinking, thinking even the skin 'round her eyes looked grassy and her mouth was ringed with a greenish shadow but I couldn't tell for sure, there in the half-light.

—I can't help you, Mrs. Mills, though of course I'm sorry you're poorly.

—But why—

—My father is gone.

She said it just like that. Like it wasn't the strangest thing. Like the two of them hadn't been together in that house for as long as any of us had been alive.

Her dress was wet, as well as stained. I could see that now. Her dress and her hair. *The dew*, I thought. The dew and the rain the night before.

—But, Miss Ada, couldn't you just take a small look?

I knew by the way she was standing that I'd time for only one, maybe two questions. Otherwise I'd have been asking *But where has he gone, Miss Ada? Miss Ada, isn't that wet dress making you cold?*

—I'm sorry, Mrs. Mills, I hate to think of you paining, but I can't help you. I can't take Cures with Father gone.

She closed the door very gently and I thought *Cures, so that's what they call us*, and while I was standing there with the squeeze of ice in my back and all of my weight on one leg I heard her walking back through the house, heard a creak and then a tapping sound, which I knew to be the slow-swing-shut habit of the back door. Far as I know that's the last time anyone saw her. Never did figure out what happened to him.

No. My back never came right. It still gets worst right at the height of summer. Still catch myself thinking of Miss Ada, sometimes, when the summer storms come in. Catch myself near praying to her like some kind of idol.

With Father gone all these years and no Cures coming there are few habits that I keep, save tending to the sorrel leaves.

Turning over and over their slim, succulent bodies that carry their creases like much-worn leather.

Coming into summer I always mutter a haze of warning to keep at bay the lustful blood-vein moth, but still most mornings I come outside and find the leaves are ravaged. The edges robbed of their svelte curves.

I speak to them, saying their name aloud, mostly for the pleasure of the first *r* rippling into its twin.

Sorril,
Sorrelle,
Soreil.

Now that autumn is coming the sorrel has garnered a reddish hue and it cheers me, to see it peering above the gurgling foliage. Once, Father melted down the leaves and fed them to a girl born too sweet. Brown-haired child with the heady center of a sugarcane running thick in her veins. Father said only the sorrel's broth would cleanse her.

Sorrel. Meaning sour.

Meaning heartbeat quickened.

Meaning puckering tang.

*　　*　　*

At first I don't understand the sound.

It might be a felled branch; the house rhythmically creaking.

I wait on the lawn, and it comes again.

It's been so long since someone knocked on the door.

I've been outside all day and so the kitchen and the hallway feel almost too cool. It's already evening inside.

Through the screen: a youngish man, standing with his back to the house, showing me his muscled back. The vest he has on is worn thin and shows the taut flesh creasing together about the spine. Bundled together, muscles like ropes. His hair is the color of wet sand, clinging thickly to itself. Like grit. When he shakes his head at some bug come too close and turns to me a wound inside me comes open.

It is Samson's face.

Samson's face, only not quite—there's a closeness to the mouth and chin, a tightness between the eyes. Samson's shoulders, only not quite wide enough. Samson's hair but not fair enough.

Squinting through the screen. Very tall, and so ducking his head.

—Miss Ada?

I step closer and quickly he's confused. He's been expecting an old woman.

—That's right.

He's wearing a hat that shades his eyes, but I can see his jaw. It tightens, sees some of his handsomeness undone.

—I'm Olivia Wyde's son.

*   *   *

Father, his chest broad and taut as a drum.

His eyelids heavy and creasing. Speaking short bursting sentences while there was still speech inside him.

—You're sick, Ada.

On his side, his shoulders slumping and his hips weighting themselves toward the floor. In the half-light, in my confusion, I thought they were melting.

—I won't be without him.

—Sick is sick.

—There'll be no one else, you know that. No other Cure would—

—It has to fetch up somewhere.

This boy looking at me like he wants to come inside.

—My mother died a few days ago.

—I see.

—She said I should visit you.

—That so.

—She said I might talk to you about my father.

His long arms and his long legs and the freckles that frame his eyes.

What is Olivia out to do, tucked safely inside her grave?

—I've come a long way to see you.

—Come in, I say, and he opens the door himself, makes the hallway feel small. We walk through to the kitchen; I sit at the table and he shakes his head when I suggest that he do the same. He leans instead on the back of a chair, both hands gripping it, the knuckles blanching.

—I didn't hear your car.

—I parked a little ways away. Legs needed stretching.

I put a hand on my collar and rub at the divot there.

—Your mother was still young.

He makes an easy gesture, letting me know he's had his fill of grief. His hands have her quickness.

—What age was she? Fifty-two?

Slow, careful look he gives me.

—That's right, fifty-two.

I should have said fifty. Fifty-five.

He looks around the cupboards. All of them long empty.

—I wasn't sure you'd be here.

He's giving off something like Samson's scent.

—I saw you, in your mother, before you were born.

Like my tongue is unraveling down my chest. Years of quiet taking their toll. But he only says

—She told me a little about it. Said you and your father used to heal people who lived in the town.

—Yes, we saw to them . . . fixed them when we could.

—Mother said you fixed her twice, when she was having me.

I look at the window, look back at the table.

—A few days ago she told me she was always afraid to have more, once you stopped healing.

He coughs without covering his mouth and looks down at an angle to the floor.

—Or not taking on patients, rather. And anyway. We moved away.

—Father died, and I lost my gift.

—There's a jar belonging to this house in our kitchen. She kept it next to the tiled part of the wall.

Dark-eyed, watchful Olivia.

—I hope you don't think me cruel, but you seem to be coping well.

He laughs at this and moves one hand, closed in a fist, behind his back. Begins kneading at some tension there.

—We weren't particularly close. My mother was always busy.

He shifts the hair on his forehead to reveal the skin beneath. Not yet cooled, still lined with its saltwater beads.

—I don't think the town knew what to do with a single mother.

—Can't tell you how small our home seemed, even as a boy. But yes. She was a single mother.

And now: a child no longer. A young man looking down at me with anger lining his insides.

—You never saw my mother again?

I let out a breath and lean back in my chair.

—No. I don't leave the house.

—Why's that?

—I'm sick.

With loneliness. With waiting.

—I'm very sick.

—You wear it well.

He means to be cruel or to bring to the air some trace of sex.

He's too like him. They're too alike. Though Samson would have no taste for this nonsense back-and-forth. He's gotten that from her.

—Am I very different than you expected?

He straightens then and gathers the front of his vest in

his fist, smiling and rubbing it over his stomach, stretching it toward his sternum.

—I'm sorry, Miss Ada, but I've been hearing about you since I was a child—and mixed things at that. I hardly know what to think.

—Cures like to talk.

—What's that now?

—People . . . often speak nonsense. It strikes them as odd that I live here alone.

—My mother said to be wary of you.

I pick up the lap of my dress and rub my face in it, forgetting myself. When I look at him again his stubble is glinting like a brand-new coin.

—What's that?

—My mother. She said you were a little bit a witch.

My turn to laugh. I look into the garden. It must be almost time. All these years alone, and now I'm rich with company.

To get up to the attic you need to crawl on all fours. Your face comes very close to the splinters in the boards. The sound you make is like an animal with calloused feet. It's not a place where you can softly tread. No matter how small the movement or sound it comes shaking down through the whole house. So loud you expect the walls to shudder and the ceiling to shake.

Those first months alone I went into the attic often. In the summer evenings its window lets in a wedge of light that follows the sharp angle of the roof.

I'd stand and sniff at the air, getting beyond the smell

of the heap of blankets I'd nested in as a child. I felt their scratching wool catch the thin hair of my thin feet.

This was where he'd taken me when I was learning to taste, to touch and hear and see, while my skin came away in layers to leave a more weathered coating behind. The floorboards coated in a dense sweep of loam, Father making noises to teach me the rhythms of speech.

What did I look like before I looked like myself?

A huddled creature in the ground. Carried up here and permitted to grow, sleeping through the too-harsh day with Father coming up every evening. I remember his hands on me; the base of his palm a blunt instrument of measure between my legs and on the small of my back, his thumb's incremental progression along the length of my spine a means of testing each inch for cracks.

We came back to where we'd started, these last few years. The two of us in the attic, and one of us wondering what we'd done.

I'd slide down the wall and sit beside him. Study his bruised lips and his tongue limp between them.

The wound taking him over and turning him back to soil. An untended flower bed that spat up its seeds.

Tucked into the corner of the floor and the harsh slope of the wall he lay wilting—he wilted quite softly, in fact, as certain flowers do in our forsaken summer heat. His skin was the heaving droplet hang of their saddened petals.

Until the very end, a sound came out of him.

A chord from a song I didn't recognize.

Just the one chord, over and over.

For a time I thought he wanted to tell me something, to

scold me, hurt me, to follow me through the house and remind me of what I'd done.

But now I don't think that he could help it or that he even felt it happening. Now I think the song was lodged so deep inside him—that the whole of him, his length and breadth, was threaded through and through with so much song—that his flesh carried on producing it.

For years, the sound of it.

And then silence.

Until today, and this knocking at the door.

Tall, fair boy. Looking down at me with a cautious kind of pity. I pull at my hem.

—So it's not true?

—What?

—You're not a witch.

—Do I look like a witch?

—No, but it's what my mother said and she didn't often lie.

Before I can stop myself, I laugh. Quick, dry sound. An alien feeling in my throat. It offends him and he stands a fraction straighter.

—When I was little she said you were a monster I'd one day have to kill. She said you murdered my daddy.

—Someone murdered your daddy but it wasn't me.

Thinking of Olivia leaning over Harry with a pillow, mixing into his coffee some vial of poison. But he ignores me, says

—I couldn't sleep most nights, when I was little, thinking of you. She said you murdered him so you could eat him, and that I had to kill you. That if I killed you he'd jump right out of your stomach.

And now he looks at my stomach, the slight bulge where my dress is sticking.

—But look at you. A girl.

A contempt for females. That too he's gotten from her.

—The real Miss Ada. The first one. She was your sister? Your mother?

My breath is sore now, in my chest. I haven't spoken this much in so long.

—Your mother was under a lot of strain, with Harry dying, and then her brother—

—Who's Harry?

Mist-like evening light. Denying the storm and its promise of rain. I am afraid that if I look away for too long he'll come up and simply walk away, that The Ground will have leeched his memory and he won't know I'm here, waiting.

—Your father. Your mother's husband.

He creases his eyes and his nose follows.

—My father's name was Samson.

He seems to be getting larger, blocking the door to the hall.

—And my mother had no brother.

There's something wrong with me. I wish you'd look inside.

And Olivia's hand flaring across her stomach and the unborn baby inside.

Flared large and white like a sheet caught on the line.

*   *   *

There was a stain on one of the blankets; its pale yellow corner seemed to have been dipped in a red and purple dye, and I recalled then, as I hadn't for a time, how Father had once spooned mulch into my soundless mouth. A little jar he'd bring up with him, and sit next to me with a silver spoon seeming twig-like in his hand.

—Eat, Ada, and you'll soon be strong.

There'd been an evening when he had left me to feed myself, and unable to use the spoon I'd dipped the blanket's bunched corner into the jar and held it there till it was full and sopping, and then I suckled from it. The coarse cloth slow to give up its heady brew. I'd a name for it, I remember, the first words I ever strung: *Blueberry sediment crush*, because Father had said it would nestle inside me and if ever anyone saw inside me all they'd see would be blueberry after blueberry, wet and purple and red. Sitting with the blanket tugged into my lap I marveled at how well the color kept: bright, bold stain I hadn't been able to lift with the small pocket of my mouth.

Later, when he came back, he sat down with his back against the wall and said that he himself had never cared for the unseemly shape of spoons.

—I'm here to ask you where my father is. She said you'd know.

—Why didn't she come herself?

Now he shrugs. I'm asking him things he's asked himself.

—She said it wasn't the right time.

—Seems a funny thing to wait on.

—Where is he?

He tried to tell me. Over and over he tried to tell me.

Sick is sick. It has to go somewhere. And now here is this boy with his china cup cheekbones and his almond eyes.

No wonder The Ground is churning.

—I think you should go now. Maybe come back another time.

—She said to come soon as she died, and now she's dead.

—There's nothing I can do for you.

Something I'd seen but wouldn't look at.

That short-tailed animal with its bloodied snout.

Hands in his back pockets, vaulting his chest. He might try to hit me. He's picturing it, at least.

—Why would she lie?

—I can't answer for your mother.

Shifting his weight like the floor is hot. Looking over my head, teeth grating.

—I've been in town a few days, you know. Asking around about you, and . . . Why didn't you say you had company?

He is looking behind me, where the garden holds the evening's fading light.

—You should go.

—He . . .

Because of course, even at this distance, he can see the resemblance between them. Not so changed, then. Not on the outside. I watch his face, his temples crowding. Turning to creases the soft skin between his eyes.

—Come back another time.

—Who is he?

Headed for the back door, his face open as a child's. The sadness he must've felt as a boy in want of a father, all flooding back now and making bright pools of his eyes.

—Don't. Don't go outside.

Olivia sent me their son, to let me know he lied to me.

Thinking she'd change my mind.

Probably she'd thought the two of us have been living together all these years, taking our supper at the same time every evening, and couldn't help herself. Probably scrawled a map to the house right as she died.

But I should be thankful. Must be this boy who's pulled him up. The closeness of this poor, ignorant boy.

And besides.

Olivia forgot: I'm no Cure.

There's little I can't abide.

His feet are heavy in his boots as he walks past me.

The rain is coming. I know already the patterned indentations it'll leave on the lawn.

He will be much changed, I know, after all these years in The Ground.

In the garden, his son's voice cracking:

—Who are you?

In the garden, his legs all tremble.

—What's your name?

Much changed.

The door swinging shut. Wind coming in. Lamp set to squeak.

You'll get hurt, I might say. I might say, *Run home and stay there.*

Who knows what he's been stewing in.

Who knows what I've made.

—I said, what's your name?

All that matters: he'll be more like me.

—Tell me—

Father said over and over it wouldn't work.

Said over and over it wouldn't sit right.

He thought he'd plant regret in me and I'd try to bring him up myself, maim or kill him with him half out of The Ground.

But I've only grown more certain.

Have only grown more sure.

Nothing is too much for the scratch of hair on his chest and the gleam of his cheeks when he turns his face toward flat, hard sunshine.

No matter if he's strange. No matter if he's been birthed with a flicker he hadn't before. No matter if he's cruel or governed by a hungry fever. No matter, because I'll no longer be sat here with my heart unseeded and my insides crackling dry.

So long, too long, in the desert.

Acknowledgments

This book has received countless kinds of support over the years, but especial, enormous thanks to Dan Bolger, Mariel Deegan, and everybody at New Island Books for their initial belief in my work, and to the Arts Council for supporting the novel at its earliest stages. Thank you to Megan Mayhew Bergman and the entirety of my Bennington family. Thank you to Dan and Téa for their transatlantic (and often incredibly timely) support. Thank you to Fiona Murphy and Jane Lawson at Doubleday, and to Sally Howe at Scribner. Thank you to Amelia Atlas. A thousand times thank you to Lucy Luck for proving such an inexhaustible champion. Thank you to Dave and Jonelle, for keeping my head and heart in such good shape, to my Dublin women, without whom I would be very much alone, to my parents and my sister for their tireless, matter-of-fact support, and to my partner for reading—with enthusiasm—every single draft.

About the Author

Sue Rainsford is a fiction and arts writer based in Dublin. A graduate of Trinity College, Dublin, and Dún Laoghaire Institute of Art, Design and Technology, in January 2017 she completed her MFA in writing and literature at Bennington College, Vermont. She is a recipient of the VAI/DCC Critical Writing Award, the Arts Council Literature Bursary Award, and a MacDowell Colony Fellowship. When it was first published by New Island Books, *Follow Me to Ground* won the Kate O'Brien Award and was longlisted for the Desmond Elliott Prize and the Republic of Consciousness Prize.

31901067103939